Raised in NYC by an eccentric British father and a sometime-model mother, Peggi Davis had an unusual and more-than-memorable childhood. She earned a degree in communication arts from Texas A & M University, Commerce. She then entered the world of retail advertising. Her tenure as fashion art director, and ultimately, a national award-winning creative director, spanned the country's major department stores to NYC's Madison Avenue. Her acclaimed memoir *Funny Face* was awarded the 2022 Nonfiction Book Award and Readers' Favorite 2022 International Book Award for Nonfiction/Comedy. She currently resides in Birmingham, Alabama.

This story is dedicated to all the sassy seniors who realize that aging is a privilege, not a promise.

Peggi Davis

REWIND RANCH

AUSTIN MACAULEY PUBLISHERS™

LONDON * CAMBRIDGE * NEW YORK * SHARJAH

Ordering Information
Quantity sales: Special discounts are available on quantity purchases by corporations, associations, and others. For details, contact the publisher at the address below.

Publisher's Cataloging-in-Publication data
Davis, Peggi
Rewind Ranch

ISBN 9798889103912 (Paperback)
ISBN 9798891554634 (Hardback)
ISBN 9798889103929 (ePub e-book)

Library of Congress Control Number: 2023915466

www.austinmacauley.com/us

First Published 2024
Austin Macauley Publishers LLC
40 Wall Street, 33rd Floor, Suite 3302
New York, NY 10005
USA

mail-usa@austinmacauley.com
+1 (646) 5125767

It is with great humility and gratitude that I credit the ladies of 2600 for providing the inspiration for this story. As a small, Southern condominium community, we share the best of times and the worst of times. And somehow through it all we manage to laugh out loud.

Your friendship means the world to me.

Table of Contents

Chapter 1
The Ladies of 777

The condo coffee klatch convened daily in the trendy taupe lobby of 777 Wexford.

It was a small group of geriatrics, composed of four older and much wealthier female residents, of the city's newest and most luxurious condominium building. And the only one with a concierge, who graciously greeted them daily by name, and complimented whatever they happened to be wearing. It felt more like a boutique hotel, with the exception of no room service, with amenities included for everything else.

And its gigantic gas lanterns that flooded the massive glass and stone entrance with light warmly welcomed residents and guests alike with a feeling of safety, security, and style. It was the address that raised eyebrows at luncheons and dramatic donations at charity dinners. It sat majestically on the sunny corner of historical Highgrove Park Avenue, across from a beautifully manicured, bucolic park, and was Birmingham, Alabama's answer to New York's Upper East Side and San Francisco's Pacific Heights.

As in all small communities, residents tended to gather in groups of common interest and age. The Wexford was a mixed bag, housing a large group of young professionals and physicians who worked at the nearby medical center. There were several widows and widowers, divorcees and divas who downsized as they do when becoming a household of one, and a few couples who moved as they transitioned to empty nesters. Most newcomer conversations began with a recap of the square footage of their last home instead of the size of their genitals, but the message was the same: "I am something special." Luckily, their fading eyesight enshrouded the rush of rolling eyeballs as they spoke.

But there were some who didn't feel special anymore; that small group of female friends who sat on the smooth leather sofas as the newbies mingled. Three of them had grown up together and had been besties until the lure of college took them in different directions. As their lives unfolded, all three returned home and ultimately to the sought-after Wexford Condominium.

A few years later, at the insistence of one of the girls, a Texas transplant joined them as well. Four wealthy women who had seen better days and much better nights gathered each morning for a catch-up and communal conversation before planning their day. They took turns bringing the libations and a tray of freshly toasted muffins as they traded stories and secrets like sorority sisters and became a consciously coupled clan.

After several months of tall Bloody Mary's, they came to realize that they shared a distinct common goal. They wanted to feel young and beautiful again. They missed being admired, by men and women alike, as they had in their near-perfect, pampered pasts.

Or maybe 'desired' was the word.

All the ladies had a different expression of longing, but it meant the same thing. They were invisible, and they didn't like it. Oh sure, they had weathered their eye jobs and facelifts, doing their best to hide their bruised and bloated lids and jowls. And they had monthly Botox and fillers and their SilverSneakers classes at the gym. But, despite all this, they still looked worn for wear. "Great for their age," people kindly remarked. "Handsome but not beautiful."

Horses are handsome.

So they deflected their fears through friendships fraught with the angst of aging. A tight, exclusive clique that shared the building's gossip and glory, the four women ate lunch at the country club and drank dinner alone at home. They had married well, divorced better, and some wonderfully widowed. They were all single, successful, financially secure, and smart. But, as life would have it, they couldn't seem to turn back time. No Benjamin Buttons in this group.

So they played bridge and mahjong and vinyl records from the past, dreaming of the days when they were desired by many. They languished over past luncheons where the conversation would stop as they entered the room. Dressed to the nines in three-inch heels, they couldn't care less what they ate. No white; no sugar; no bubbles. It was an easy way to weigh less than their tablemates who couldn't resist gobbling down their chicken casserole and crème brûlée.

Little did they know that in the near future, there would appear a solution, a miracle of sorts, that would change their lives into a fantasy they could never imagine. That their days of games and gin fizzes would become much, much better, and the four freshly painted walls of the Wexford lobby would be replaced by a world that they never knew existed.

But not today.

Today, they had things to do and places to go. Their calendars were filled with as many appointments as necessary to pass the time. Hair, nails, and of course the gym. Maybe a quick dip in the pool when it was all clear. Their snug-skirted swimsuits did their best to hide the soft folds of flesh being pulled by gravity toward the cool concrete decking.

They couldn't risk being seen, especially by the few handsome divorcees and widowers who occupied most of the one-bedroom units. They were lucky to have such a nice selection of sophisticated Southern suitors about, just in case an evening escort was needed. It never went beyond that. Even though they were almost all age-appropriate, they seemed to be surrounded by much younger ladies in skin-tight, thigh-high dresses that resembled their well-hidden SPANX underwear. "Utterly disgusting," the four women whispered to each other.

They vetted prospective newcomers with surgical precision, trying to blackball anyone who was not of their class. It was an old Southern caste system basically based on family and funds. It helped if you belonged to the country club, lived in the right neighborhood, and, of course, dressed the part. No Birkenstocks allowed here. Being 'well-read' in this group referred to the color of your savvy shoe soles.

Most ladies were locals. Raised in the toniest of townships, all preferential high school sorority selects and a few obvious Homecoming Queens, they scattered when college became their focus. Lacey Ann was accepted to the prestigious American Ballet Theatre Studio Company in New York and Mary Grace to Georgetown.

Margot went to the state's favorite University of Alabama. Soon elected sorority president, she bonded with the Texas transplant Elizabeth 'Elli' Johnson during rush week. When Elli pledged, Margot grabbed her as her Little Sis. Tall, trim, and tan, they were the envy of most girls in the house, much less the entire UA campus. Margot majored in French, thinking it would be beneficial in restaurants and on vacations, while Elli honed her design skills, hoping to become an art director for a top fashion magazine in New York, a dream she had since her discovery of *Seventeen Magazine* years ago.

She was ambitious and worked hard in the afternoons at the school library to afford her art supplies and sorority dues. Sometimes, she modeled for the life-drawing classes in the evenings. What Elli didn't have in cents, she had in determination and style.

So like the shining stars in the universe, the fabulous four converged many years later in a luxury condominium in Birmingham, Alabama. Their lives had been as diverse as a pot of gumbo that slowly simmered and melded together like magic. They had decades of stories to tell; some of laughter, some of loss. But these gals weren't tied to the past emotionally. They were determined to savor their last years and live life to the absolute fullest. They just hadn't figured out how.

One afternoon at another wine-infused lunch, the ladies decided a trip was in order. Maybe to an island, maybe to a spa, or maybe even a cruise. It was turning spring time and the girls had been obsessed with shopping for colorful caftans and woven straw slides.

"Maybe Greece," Margot suggested. "Sailing the Mediterranean is marvelous, and the fresh fish is fabulous!"

"And the shopping on Hydra is the absolute best," chimed in Mary Grace.

"My passport is expiring. It will be months before I'll get it back," lamented Lacey Ann, "and the crowds along Rosemary Beach are a nightmare this time of year. Maybe the Florida Keys?"

"Boring," immediately groaned the group. "We want adventure, beauty, men with six packs!"

"Okay, okay. Everyone, please research some ideas, and we can talk about them at the end of the week. But we can't go until next month. I have my little refresh scheduled with Dr. McDreamy next week," reminded Margot. "We must keep our priorities straight."

And, so after lunching on paper-thin slices of carpaccio and chilled asparagus soup, the ladies went their separate ways. Some to the gym, some to the shops, and one to her home computer to find the perfect vacation. It had to be exceptional; the vacation of a lifetime, and one they would certainly never forget. It was a hard task for this group; they were all well-traveled.

They had safaried in Botswana and walked the Great Wall in China. They had skied the Alps and swum in the blue lagoons of Thailand. What on earth was left? And without a passport no less. This was going to take some real creativity and keen detective work, and it won't be close to cheap. But they had made a pact and adopted a mantra, 'at our age, say yes to everything'.

The answer came quite unexpectedly the following week as Margot was paying for her time-altering touch-up with Dr. McDreamy. That wasn't his real name, of course, but one assigned to him by the group. Easy to talk to, and on the eyes as well, he had become a favorite among the vintage vino crowd.

Tall, dark, and handsome, the forty-something physician was not only a medical marvel but also had an artist's eye that instinctively knew the perfect places to inject. "As with art," he lectured one day, "it's all about the light and its reflection; disguising shadows and lines that reveal the reality of aging."

At the clinic's check-out counter sat a colorful brochure that caught Margot's slightly swollen eyes. On the cover was a photograph of an exquisite, exotic, elderly woman lying on a sandy white beach. Her skin was flawless, the color of café au lait that glowed like glass in the sunlight. Her hair was blowing in the breeze in sheets of shining satin, and she emitted an aura of pure pleasure, of being perfectly content and confident.

The brochure was advertising the newest concept in destination resorts, a place to become as beautiful as your heart desired while living a life of pure, hedonistic luxury. It was a pristine, palatial campus of sorts, with a massive white stucco hotel and adjoining spa, and a state-of-the-art medical center staffed with surgeons from all around the world.

There was a white sand beach for sunning, an infinity pool for swimming, and unlimited classes in yoga, Pilates, hair and make-up, fashion styling, nutrition, and relationships. It was a ranch, of sorts, breeding and raising thoroughbreds, and a soothing sunset ride on the beach was a finger snap away. There were six restaurants, a 1980s discotheque, and two jazz clubs. Their activity calendar, published in the resort's newsletter and delivered to your room at breakfast, announced each evening's activities. These ranged from the coolest concerts to a calm and carefree version of speed dating that somehow incorporated complementary and chilled bottles of Dom Pérignon.

It was an all-inclusive, extremely exclusive, pleasure-seeking paradise for older men and women. Covering over three hundred acres on the remote side of Maui, the Hana-based property promised perfectly prepared meals, sound-proofed sleeping suites, unlimited classes and cocktails, matches and mixers, and a roster of plastic surgeons, cosmetic dentists, and runway stylists to create the you of your dreams. The before and after photos were absolutely staggering. It was the first of its kind in the entire world; a paradise on earth, where you could stay as long as you wish.

It was a dream come true, and it was called Rewind Ranch.

Of course, it was pricey. Not a terrible problem for the three originals, but Elli might not be able to swing the expense. Margot noticed that there were three levels of entry fees, though, once your application was accepted. How interesting that you had to be voted worthy of entrance to drop hundreds of thousands of dollars. *'But it would keep out the riffraff,'* she thought, and was grateful that no children or anyone under sixty was even allowed.

And some people seemed to stay forever, giving up their safe, sensible lives back home in the cornfields of Iowa or other godforsaken places. There were testimonials from a dozen or so guests; women regally resembling the marvelous model Carmen Dell'Orefice and a group of men who could have easily passed for Rock Hudson or Paul Newman.

Margot couldn't wait to get home to study the brochure. She needed to be totally knowledgeable before she presented it to the girls. It would be easy to grab their interest but may be a hard sell financially. It was a lot of money for even them, fixed incomes and all. But, with the tiered memberships, surely, they all could swing it. At worst, they could have a new face and body, a premier match introduction, and two weeks in paradise at the Silver level.

Gold members stayed six weeks plus better accommodations, three premier matches, and preferred seating at all events. But it was the Platinum Circle that peeked Margot's interest. Not only would she get all the Gold level perks, but six glorious months in heaven with a dozen premier matches with male guests, a nomination to become the island's hallowed Harvest Queen, and a chance to become a permanent resident of the resort.

Feeling fully refreshed and tingling with excitement, Margot put her shiny new Mercedes in gear and backed out of her parking space. Looking in the rearview mirror, she checked the tiny red puncture marks on her face. She would need to stay in today, all the better to research this lucky, life-altering trip. Margot felt it was kismet, karma, a divine intervention. She felt it in her bones, with an absolute dead certainty.

Chapter 2
Margot Meadows

With a bigger-than-life personality, she was the It Girl of the Tiny Kingdom.

Attractive, athletic, and admired, Margot Meadows was the envy of almost every female student in her tony township's high school. Born to privileged parents and an only child at that, young, fresh-faced Margot was spoiled rotten. Her extracurricular activities and awards were second only to her grade point average. Smart and studious, the young teen was destined to be a success. As class president, cheer captain, and the state's star tennis champion, Margot was more than comfortable in the limelight. Being the center of attention was a normal state of affairs for her, and she became an 'influencer' way before the word was even invented.

Needless to say, she was never without a Friday night date and played the field with the expertise of Mata Hari. But her dreams were much larger than a football captain or star lacrosse player from Alabama. Yes, Margot had a plan. Primed by her uber-successful parents, she knew from a very young age that the world was her oyster. It was just a matter of netting the one with the pearl.

Her valedictorian commencement speech was aired on local television news shows. There stood Margot, like a shining star at the podium in her perfectly pressed cap and gown, her blonde hair slightly swaying in the breeze, her bright blue eyes sparkling with enthusiasm and excitement. No notes, no slipups, no nonsense. She encouraged everyone to follow their hearts, accomplish their wildest dreams, and plan to make the world a better place for generations to come. She received a standing ovation, and her photo was on the front page of the treasured town's weekly circular.

Her parents, Kim and Skipper Meadows, were over the moon.

After a lovely reception of sweet tea and school-crested cookies on the school's landscaped lawn, the jubilant Meadows family headed toward the country club for a secret, celebratory luncheon for their distinguished daughter Margot and her two best friends: Lacey Ann Peyton and Mary Grace Caldwell. The three well-heeled friends had grown up together in the same splendid neighborhood and were a closed clique all the way through school.

Their parents socialized together whether it was chairs of the city's many charity galas or summers at the state's beautiful white sand beaches where they all owned second, shingled salt-box homes. The girls were all legacies to the city's best high school sorority, a Southern social staple, and of course were selected to join as soon as they hit the ninth grade.

All pretty and popular, they composed sought-after honors and titles throughout their education. Most Beautiful, Most Likely to Succeed, Homecoming Queen, Fraternity Sweetheart—you name it, they won it. The Trifecta, as they were known around town, were a feckless force to be reckoned with. And, naturally, unflinching, undaunted Margot was the leader of the pack.

The luncheon was a big hit.

Swathed in Alabama Crimson Tide red and white balloons and streamers, the reserved restaurant room was ablaze with Margot's favorite school colors. The round table in the center, with an unblemished view of the aqua-blue swimming pool, was accessorized with a clear vase of white peonies with matching corsages at each place setting. The girls gasped as they entered, and Kim Meadows grinned ear to ear at their awestruck response to her decorating ideas.

The club had followed her instructions implicitly, something the $4,000-a-month dues guaranteed. "Perfection every day in every way" was their motto. It was embroidered on the waitstaff's jackets and silk-screened on the T-shirts of the trainers, lifeguards, landscapers, and masseuses.

She had selected the Southern chicken salad plate, complete with fresh fruit salad and a warm orange roll for their meal, but first had arranged for a champagne toast. She wondered if it was the girls' first taste of good champagne. Probably not, as the many wild weekend parties at their parents' homes would surely have resulted in a few popped corks. Her husband, Skipper, probably slipped them a case. Today, he raised his empty glass and gave a tearful toast instead.

"May you celebrate your graduation remembering special memories from your past and exciting dreams for your future."

"To the Trifecta," the giddy girls added, "may we marry well and divorce better." Everyone laughed except Mrs. Meadows. Somehow, their high school attempt at humor didn't even get a chuckle out of her.

The meal was delicious, followed by a beautiful serving of strawberry shortcake, also red and white, made fresh for them that morning. The luncheon was filled with both laughter and nostalgia as the girls were each going their separate ways. After several whoops of 'Roll Tide!', the girls gathered their things and walked arm in arm to the club's main entrance as Mr. Meadows skipped ahead and quickly approached the vigilant valet.

Moments later, a brand new, bright red Mercedes convertible drove up topped with a huge white bow attached to its hood. "Happy graduation, kitten," quipped Mr. Meadows as he softly touched Margot's tawny shoulder. The girls shrieked in shock and surprise as he opened the driver's door for his cherished daughter as the other two jumped in. A large grin covered his fleshy face as the Trifecta peeled off in a cloud of dust hiding the vanity plate just attached that morning. It said 'Roll Tide'.

With the radio turned up full blast, the trio sang *Lollipop* by the Chordettes and the somewhat taboo *Good Golly, Miss Molly* by Little Richard, a musician their moms deemed unfit for nice, young Southern girls. They felt the same way about that hip-swinging, rock-and-roll-singing Elvis Presley and preferred the smooth voices of the whitewashed, wasp-friendly Everly Brothers and the Kingston Trio.

Of course, Margot's mom was enthralled with Elvis. She'd never seen anything like him. He stirred feelings inside her from long, long ago; way before her practically arranged marriage to the slightly overweight, but in line for a fat inheritance, Skipper Meadows, the town's most eligible bachelor. His nickname came from his love of sailing, a hobby that afforded him a number of bikini-clad beach babes before he supposedly settled down. Seems he ended up Kim's escort to every deb ball she attended, as she was introduced to Birmingham's booming society, most of which were held at this very same country club.

Soon, it would be Margot's turn to grace the society page at her debut. But, first, she had to get through college, joining the right sorority and the right clubs and dating the right young men. College was more a rite of passage for moneyed Southern girls, hardly preparatory for a profession. They laughed when they said they earned a Mrs. degree, but it was hardly a joke. The challenge was to earn it without getting pregnant; a fate worse than death at that age and station.

Most girls moved away, destined for a life void of Birmingham's bustling society scene…the cliques, the cocktails, the clubs. Returning to the Tiny Kingdom as a young, upwardly mobile couple was the goal, something never spoken but intrinsically understood. Those not as lucky were greeted at the local pharmacy or Piggly Wiggly with a stiff smile and an uncomfortable utterance of, "How are you, dear?" knowing full well the more accurate speculation was one of complete horror and a silent acknowledgment of her terrible luck or lack of planning. This exclamation and encounter would then be broadcast to a circle of colleagues who would lament the lackluster life and futile future of the girl in question, followed by an hour-long discussion on the virtues of being a virgin, or being extremely careful if you're not.

The latter covered most of the senior class.

Chapter 3
Elli Jane Johnson

Elizabeth Jane Johnson lived on the wrong side of town.

Born in Galveston, Texas, her parents moved to the gleaming metropolis of Dallas when she entered high school. She missed the sun-drenched beach, the undulating waves of the mighty Gulf, and the smell of salt in the air. But, most of all, she missed her friends. And she hated being the new girl in a school so large she had repetitive nightmares of being unable to find her classrooms. Luckily, she had her mother's looks and didn't go unnoticed in the first day's school assembly, a welcoming of sorts, and an encouragement to get involved in extracurricular activities.

Previously popular at Galveston Junior High, Elli wondered if she had just been a big fish in a small pond. She had been lucky to make the cheer team a few years back and with her small frame was always picked for the top of the pyramid, the team's grand finale. Her confidence was boosted by their all-state trophy from last year's competition, so she bit her lip and turned up for her new school's tryouts.

The newcomer was amazed at the group already there: probably thirty or more girls all looking like the girls she saw in her favorite

Seventeen Magazine. Their long hair was gathered in perky ponytails and their necks entwined in sassy school-colored scarves. Unfortunately, she had been born with bright red hair, something she would later embrace. But she had endured constant teasing by her classmates and was used to being called 'carrot top' and other ego-numbing names.

Elli wondered how long it would take for this bunch to do the same although the girls seemed much more sophisticated than her Galveston gang. They wore Bobbie Brooks sweater sets, pleated skirts, and the latest fad of Bass Weejuns unlike her scuffed brown oxfords and colored cotton socks. Elli almost left the gym before the practice began. Now sweating profusely, she gathered her courage and positioned herself on the very back row.

After a few run-throughs, Elli had the words and choreography down and waited her turn to perform in front of the judges, composed of Miss Walker, the stern-looking PE teacher; Miss Jacobs, the cheer squad coach; and Sandy Thomas, last year's head cheerleader. Sandy made a point of winking at all her girlfriends as they lined up alphabetically.

The competition seemed stiff as girls cartwheeled and flipped to center stage to perform their routine. She almost missed her cue when the coach called out, "Elizabeth, you're next." It hadn't occurred to her that she would have to correct everyone to call her Elli, a nickname given to her by her runaway father.

Soon it was obvious that the local girls were no match for Elli's strong legs, honed and toned from running long laps on the beach every morning. She ended her cheer with a toe-touch jump followed by a standing backflip. You could have heard a pin drop.

Selections would be posted the next day, so Elli grabbed her bulging book bag and headed out to walk the few blocks home. Nobody even acknowledged her presence, much less complimented her on her peppy, near-perfect performance. *'It's hell being invisible,'* she thought, as she grabbed her new books and headed out the gymnasium door.

August in Dallas can be hotter than a jalapeno pepper, and today was no different.

As she walked down the neighborhood streets, cars loaded with laughing teens and blaring radios passed her by. She concentrated on the houses, all tiny ranch styles with adjoining carports, and street names beginning with the Spanish word 'San'. This was East Dallas, filled with hardworking families who used public transportation and swam in city swimming pools.

She had seen other areas from the downtown bus window, much more manicured than this, with large homes surrounded by iron fences and gates enclosing giant grass lawns so green they looked like the golf course back home. Her favorite area so far was Highland Park, filled with beautiful two-story homes and immense, immaculate gardens. Her favorite street was named Turtle Creek, a beautiful winding boulevard whose median was bursting with beautiful, blooming flowers, along a pristine park complete with a small, sparkling creek and a family of ducks swimming gracefully on the water. It seemed like heaven on earth to her.

'Someday,' Elli thought.

But, today, she had learned a few lessons, the first of which was she needed to get a job and dress like the other city girls. And she needed to join more organizations and make a few friends, at least someone to sit with in the school cafeteria. Being new was lonely, and scary, and shattered your self-confidence. There was nothing worse than wandering the room alone laden with a lunch tray, as tables filled with groups of giggling girls avoided eye contact with you.

Opening the front door with her new Big D key ring, Elli put her books in her little blue bedroom and grabbed a soda out of the fridge. Time to hit the books before her mom arrived home from work. She needed to start preparing dinner, but right now, studying was her priority. She was determined to acquire a college scholarship in art and design and get out of this hell hole. That seemed much more important than frying a bunch of chicken legs.

Later that night as she lay in the tiny twin bed that consumed most of her bedroom, Elli said a prayer asking God for a friend. One friend (she didn't want to appear greedy) and a sign that her life wouldn't always be a struggle. Her mom did the best she could, and she was so appreciative, but Elli wanted more. As she drifted off to sleep, she just knew down deep that she was destined for bigger things, but just in case, she thought a tiny prayer couldn't hurt.

The next morning, the air at the school was thick with tension and excitement as students gathered around the gymnasium bulletin board before the first bell summoned them to class. As Elli slowly maneuvered through the curious crowd, she caught a glimpse of the six names posted on the cracked corkboard. And there, at the very bottom of the list, was printed the name 'Elizabeth Jane Johnson'.

Stupefied students were quietly questioning who Elizabeth Johnson could be and how in the world she managed to win a spot on the coveted cheer team. Elli swelled with joy. Finally, something good happened here. She vowed to be the best cheerleader on the squad and show these city kids who's who.

It was on that day that the unnoticed, overwhelmed, copper-topped newcomer became a force to be reckoned with at Hilltop High. It only took a few Friday night football games, a couple of successful track meets, and an article in the school newspaper written and illustrated by its newest staff member, Elli Johnson, for the students to realize that the invisible new girl was stronger, smarter, and sassier than all of them put together.

She graduated first in her class, majoring in art, and was awarded a full-tuition scholarship to the state school of her choice. Her favorite aunt happened to live in Tuscaloosa, Alabama, home of the University of Alabama's famed football team, the Crimson Tide. And, because she wanted to get away and was offered the lovely guest room for as long as she wished, Elli packed up the old faded Ford, gifted to her for graduation, and headed due east to one of the country's most scenic Southern states. And her life was never the same.

It was there that she met Margot Meadows, during a faux-friendly sorority mixer, which basically meant that the members were eyeing and judging the newbies desperately wanting an invitation. But, with Elli's bright red hair, outstanding school honors, and chic Dallas duds, it was inevitable that she would be noticed. Especially by their invincible and invaluable president, Margot Meadows.

Margot and Elli bonded immediately and were inseparable during their college years. Eventually rooming together, Margot was the sorority source for dates to any fraternity party the sisters wanted to attend. As Sweetheart of Sigma Chi, Margot had a bevy of boys from whom to choose there. And, before being pinned to Carter Winslow, the fraternity president, Margot had dated someone in every frat house on campus.

Elli, who majored in art and design, spent long hours at the Arts Building, learning the fundamentals and techniques needed to graduate with a degree. The school focused on fine arts, not commercial, so Elli realized that once graduated, she would have to learn on the job, intern if possible, in order to fulfill her dream of designing for a major fashion magazine. She sent out resumes to dozens of open positions in Birmingham, Atlanta, and Dallas and received a few less-than-exciting responses.

After several interviews, an extremely gracious creative director explained the hiring process and gave her the name of an advertising recruiter who could help her find a job. It proved to be the best advice she had been given. There were several openings in Manhattan, and Elli promptly sent her portfolio and resume to the headhunter for review. A week later, she found herself checking into a small midtown hotel, the night before her interview at a catalog design firm a few blocks away. She was thrilled that her trip was all expenses paid.

Elli was beside herself with nerves as she entered the skyscraper on Madison Avenue, her college portfolio under her arm. Maybe designing a cheap sportswear catalog wasn't *Vogue Magazine*, but it was a start. The headhunter she was working with explained that in order to be competitive in New York, she had to amass a well-edited portfolio of published work.

The agency seeking a junior art director handled a multitude of direct-mail publications, many of which were advertising fashion of some sort. They were seeking someone trainable and willing to work long hours. They also mentioned that the client 'was difficult', which was definitely a red flag. But Elli needed a job, so she was determined to make it work. The offices were beautiful; straight out of *Architectural*

Digest. She introduced herself to a dauntingly dismissive receptionist and took a seat along a line of fresh-faced, extremely thin models who were hoping for work as well.

Eventually, a tall, lanky young man with an enormous dragon tattoo circling his right arm emerged from the huge double doors of the offices. Scanning the line of ladies before him, he quickly caught Elli's eye and extended a hand. She realized she stood out because she was dressed in a business suit recently purchased at TJ Max, and not the trendy torn blue jeans and tiny white tees worn by everyone else. She looked like their mother.

"Elli? I'm Zack, creative director of the Chadburn catalog. Come with me."

This was the beginning of a lifelong friendship as Zack took Elli under his tattooed wing and trained her in catalog design and photo art direction. She also learned a great deal about politics, as 'the client', she was told, 'is always right'. They paid the bills, so it was your job to either let them or make them think they were always right. It took all Elli's patience to deal with the Chadburn team, a small group of large-size mean girls who relished telling her what to do.

Two years later, she was moved to a more prestigious team within the company, a specialty retailer in Los Angeles whose clientele were always at some red-carpet award show. The budgets were bigger, the clothes full of glitz and glam, and for the first time, Elli worked with A-list models and photographers and was exposed to real fashion photography. It wasn't long before she was selected to fill a fashion stylist position at *Elle Magazine* and eventually worked her way up the ladder to creative director. It was her life's ambition, and she did it.

Retiring at sixty years of age, Elli realized the Big Apple held no allure without her career and decided a relocation was in order. With her mother gone, it was a fluke that her college bestie, Margot Meadows, randomly called to say hello, and suggested she consider coming to Birmingham. There Elli could relax and retire in the lush location, enjoy the city's famous food scene, and join in the adventures and antics of Margot Meadows and her two close childhood chums, Lacey Ann Peyton and Mary Grace Caldwell. She would love it.

Chapter 4
Mary Grace Caldwell

Mary Grace Caldwell was born with a silver tea set in her mouth.

Her family's name was etched into hospital wings, park entrances, and university buildings around town. She grew up in an enormous English Tudor complete with nannies, cooks, and parents who spent more time at black-tie parties than with her. Despite the lack of warmth in her home, Mary Grace was a model student, kind, generous, and well-liked. It didn't hurt that she resembled gorgeous gamin Audrey Hepburn with her fragile figure, impish haircut, and enormous brown eyes that slanted up at the corners.

Those enchanting eyes were always accentuated with Maybelline's sable brown liquid liner, just like in the magazines. "Beautiful inside and out," they would say as she floated down the hallways. It was not surprising that she was voted Miss Everything in the senior class. She learned very early on, from her beloved nanny Eula, "That you catch more flies with honey."

Obviously, it worked. Mary Grace caught the eye of star baseball pitcher Beau Beeson, who became her sweetheart all through high school. Beau, son of the town's moneyed founder of the legendary law firm Beeson & Brown, assumed he and Mary Grace would marry after graduation and start a family while he entered law school and eventually joined the family's firm. But, despite her mother's narrow-minded nagging 'to grab the brass ring while you can', Mary Grace had other ideas.

She wanted to change the world.

Growing up in a household with more staff than occupants, Mary Grace was unnerved by the constant deference shown to her. It was like she could do no wrong. And, although she appreciated everyone making her life so easy, she began to wonder what they really thought of her, what was said behind closed doors. She wanted to know about them as people, not 'the help', as her mother would say. Where did they live, did they have family, and why were they serving Christmas dinner to the Caldwells and not their own families?

Eula answered some of her questions as best she could, while others just got a soft sigh and a slow shake of her head. "Now Miss Mary Grace, don't you go worrying about old Eula," she would say. "I got a roof over my head, food to eat, and a good man who works very hard every chance he gets."

One afternoon, after the old city bus picked Eula up at the corner, Mary Grace jumped into her beloved Volkswagen bug and followed her. She had never been to this shocking side of town, with peeling plank houses so narrow you could almost reach across them wall to wall. The front yards, smaller than her beautiful bedroom back home, were nothing more than patches of dirt, sprinkled with weeds.

Eula slowly climbed down the steep stairs of the old battered bus and began walking up the street. Mary Grace parked, not wanting to be seen, as Eula stopped at a house on the corner. The rotting porch steps were encased in two cracked clay flower pots blooming with radiant red geraniums. Eula felt the dirt with her knotty forefinger as she cautiously climbed up the stairs, being careful not to step where they sank, and opened the faded front door.

Mary Grace was in shock. She had no idea of the poverty in which her beloved nanny lived. And to think that all these dilapidated homes were filled with families just trying to make ends meet, living day to day on meager salaries piously doled out by privileged parents who spent little time raising their children. And, somehow, the sweet, soft-spoken Eula May Davis remained grateful, diligent, and dignified and loved her as her own.

Knowing full well she could never let her parents know she had driven to the far West Side, as it was known around town, Mary Grace vowed to do something about this. Somehow, she needed to help Eula, and all the Eulas she could. This would take some thought and some planning, but the young teen knew she had a mission, one that energized her into rethinking her future plans of college.

She was naturally accepted to the University of Alabama, where her family had just completed a new wing of the nationally ranked law school, and her parents were both accomplished alumni. Her mother was consumed with Mary Grace pledging right away, reliving her golden days as campus sweetheart.

But now Mary Grace realized that wasn't what she wanted to do. She would go to Washington, D.C. and study law and become an advocate for the underserved. She would fight for the civil rights of the Eulas of the country who were forced into unfortunate futures of living in poverty and serving holiday dinners to wealthy and well-heeled families that literally had no souls.

Things had to change.

In the fall, Mary Grace entered Georgetown University, much to the chagrin of her parents.

Affluent young ladies just didn't do such a thing when their future had been so secure and safe. They married fresh-faced frat boys in navy blazers with family crests and had beautiful children to dote on. They joined country clubs and played bridge with the girls. And, of course, they were longtime legacies of the Junior League. There they would work to support various charities after lavish lunches at the club.

This would allow them peace of mind as they languished by the pool and summoned servants to bring them plates of pimento cheese sandwiches and sweet tea. Watching their weight became a major sport, just as their spouses watched the Dow. Each had their part to play in the act of perfection, publicly displayed in posh party photographs in the Tiny Kingdom's Saturday circular and the city's slick magazines stacked in all the exclusive and sophisticated village shops.

Mary Grace landed at National Airport with butterflies in her stomach and a down coat over her shoulders. She had never lived anywhere but Alabama, and the winter snowstorms she had seen on television made her realize she needed to be prepared. A distinguished-looking gentleman in a suit and tie met her in baggage claim holding a printed sign that read 'Caldwell'. After storing her luggage in the trunk, Mary Grace was zipping down George Washington Parkway toward the city's center. As they crossed the Potomac and headed toward O Street, Mary Grace wondered how far the Georgetown Law Center would be from her dorm.

Mary Grace was enamored with the beauty of the nation's capital.

Georgetown was like nothing she had ever seen; rows of red brick townhomes with glowing gas lanterns at night, abuzz with people walking the cobblestone streets during the day. At home, nobody walked anywhere, preferring the comfort of their shiny sedans. And all the homes were vertical, not low-lying estates surrounded by acreage. And the public transportation was amazing.

Riding the sleek metro was *de rigueur*, nothing like the dusty old buses in the South. Mary Grace rode it every weekend, treating herself to long days at the Smithsonian, the National Gallery, and lingering lunches on the Potomac in scenic Old Town Alexandria, just across the river from the city center. But what caught her ardent attention was the fact that all the city's museums and memorials were free, and available to everyone, just as they should be. Moving to D.C., she concluded, was the best decision she had ever made. It opened her eyes to a new way of life, where her curiosity and love of culture was both stimulated and saturated.

But her concern over Eula, and how she was supporting herself, was troublesome and worrying. She sent gifts and money whenever her budget allowed and wrote to her weekly. It also motivated Mary Grace to study harder, learn all she could, and get good grades. She was an ideal student, vocal and challenging in class, active in campus activities outside. Steadfast and determined, the little rich girl was set on success, as if her life depended on it; knowing full well that the lives of all the Eulas of the world actually did.

Upon graduation, Mary Grace took a clerkship in Washington for a judge sympathetic to the underserved communities, whose residences and schools seemed sorely lacking as opposed to the tony streets of Georgetown and Kalorama. She loved the city, the rush of adrenaline she got stepping off the Metro at Foggy Bottom on her way to work. Mary Grace chose to live in Old Town, across the Potomac from Georgetown, an idyllic conclave of federal townhouses, great restaurants, and red-bricked streets on which to wander.

And it hosted one of the best Farmer's Markets on Saturdays, where fresh fruits, flowers, and vegetables were displayed so beautifully that it was almost an assault on her senses. She also loved sitting on a bench at the edge of the river watching the ferryboats and action across the way. She felt safe there and at home.

Before returning home, she would treat herself to a steaming bowl of creamy clam chowder at a neighborhood pub perched on the wharf. Yes, Old Town was a far cry from the streets of Washington, D.C.'s Highlands, notorious for being one of the top twenty-five most dangerous neighborhoods in the country, just a stone's throw away.

After joining her sorority alumni association and an after-work gym, Mary Grace made a small group of friends that filled her weekends and nights with social events. She joined a group of girls who regularly went to the Kennedy Center for various symphonies and dance performances and became a member of Old Town's Playhouse, a small local theater that put on extraordinary performances. She also joined the Old Presbyterian Meeting House, founded in 1772, with gated family pews inscribed with the name of its inhabitants.

The tiny church cemetery included the grave of the unknown soldier from the Revolutionary War. It was all so interesting to Mary Grace, and she immediately volunteered to fix lunches on Wednesdays for the group of hungry and homeless that depended on the church's simple meal each week. Her life was full. She had a purpose and was determined to make a difference in this crazy world she lived in.

On occasion, Paul Peyton, Lacey Ann's dad, would show up in D.C. and take Mary Grace to dinner at one of Washington's finest establishments. There she would get updated on Lacey Ann's dancing career, noticing how Paul was bursting with pride. He even mentioned that Lacey Ann's company would be performing at the Kennedy Center that fall. He and Patti had already made hotel reservations at the Hay Adams, the most prominent D.C. hotel, which prided itself on hosting the highest government officials and foreign dignitaries.

It was right up Paul's alley, and he couldn't wait to snap a few selfies from Lafayette Square with the White House in the background. He also was chomping at the bit to drop in on the basement bar, Off the Record, where it was the place to be 'seen but not heard'. Who knew who he might meet down there? He even mentioned that the Meadows might come up as well, so Mary Grace should certainly plan on attending the performance with them. Of course, they would have a wonderful dinner prior.

Moving to D.C. seemed like another lifetime now.

Mary Grace was retiring from the law firm she founded twenty years ago, Grace & Fulton. It was a people's firm, branded to help the downtrodden and those who had been wronged by the justice system, which wasn't as foolproof as Mary Grace had been taught in law school. She had a wonderful career, had worked hard, helped many, and had married her law partner, Frank. But Frank Fulton had suddenly passed away from a freak auto accident and left Mary Grace despondent. She was immobilized, looking at his empty office every day, and finally, she decided to retire.

She was leaving the firm in great hands, whip-smart young lawyers with the same passion for justice as she once had. She hadn't really told any of her friends back home in Birmingham; there was too much to do. But it was time to return home and stop the everyday fight. Time to get healthy and relax and learn to enjoy the world from which she came. It would be a sorely needed fresh start, filled with lazy Southern evenings, cicadas chirping, fireflies flying, the scent of magnolias, and the glorious Southern sunsets of her youth.

As she closed the last box and flipped off the lights, Mary Grace prayed she was doing the right thing. She'd always worked hard for change and embraced change. Now it was her turn to experience change, by her choice. But it didn't feel like she had imagined.

Her stomach fluttered with butterflies in anticipation of the unknown. She had always been a lawyer, defined by her work and reputation. Now she was another single Golden Girl, returning home to live out her golden years. Without Washington's adrenaline, Mary Grace wondered how she would feel as she walked down the broken sidewalks of the shaded Southern streets. And, instead of always avoiding people's eyes, how strange it will be to smile and say 'Good morning' or stop and chat about the weather or ask about the furry friend they are leading across the street, almost void of noise and traffic. How very strange indeed.

Chapter 5
Lacey Ann Peyton

The perfectly buffed brass plate to the right of the towering front door read 'Peyton Place'.

It was her father's idea of a joke, his humor usually lost on her uptight, monotone-minded mother. Paul and Patti Peyton were an enigma; he was an attention-grabbing political figure, and she was a brilliant, devoted mother to their daughter Lacey Ann. As a young girl, Lacey often wondered what on earth brought these two together, until one day she overheard her dad laughing on the phone with an old college colleague. "Yeah, I'm living the life of luxury. Good looks on a bad boy has its advantages." It had never occurred to her that men married for money, too.

But her mom didn't seem to mind. She always glowed as they left the house for the myriad of posh parties they attended. He was a handsome man for sure and was somewhat stunning when in a tux. And, to top it off, he was always the life of the party; full of wit and wisecracks as he expounded on his past escapades and present gaffs on the golf course. Yes, Paul Peyton was the perfect politician; he could look at you like you were the only person in the universe with his glass green eyes that only wandered when a good-looking lady entered his line of sight.

Margot's mom, Kim Meadows, was that good-looking lady. Paul Peyton had been watching her at every school function and neighborhood barbecue for months. Her husband, Skipper, didn't seem very attentive, and it was Paul who always danced with Kim as their spouses were deep in conversation across the table about some silly city ordinance or the upcoming election. All that was work to him, and this was an opportunity to let loose and have fun.

Kim was hesitant at first, but when Elvis's *Jailhouse Rock* came blaring through the speakers, she just couldn't help herself. As they began to shimmy and shake to the brisk, bold beat, people cleared the dance floor to watch them. They were laughing and having fun; feeling the freedom of their youth, something neither had felt in a long, long time. When the song ended and *Love Me Tender* began to play, Paul reached for Kim's hand to pull her close.

"Oh my goodness, I have to catch my breath," she whispered. 'Just wait, little lady', Paul thought with a grin, as he reluctantly released her hand.

Lacey Ann watched with an eagle's eye as her dad and Kim Meadows returned to their spouses sitting at the long table covered in a red-and-white-checked cloth. Neither seemed to have noticed the passion play happening on the makeshift dance floor right in front of their eyes. It wasn't lost on Lacey Ann, and she made a mental note to watch more closely to learn more about her parents' marriage without being too obvious.

But she always knew, if push came to shove, her dad would never let their tight union untie. He would be lost without Patti, dull as she was, and as they say, "The man with the gold has the power." That, without question, wasn't him. And she seemed unflappable; nothing got her excited or enraged. It must be the Valium she secretly swallowed every morning.

Lacey Ann had found her stash when looking for an emery board several months ago. Being a politician's wife wasn't easy for Patti despite her interest in the issues facing Birmingham today. She was on the City Council when they met years ago and fought each other tooth and nail over public transit. He won, of course, but he admired her spunk, which somehow dissipated after she became his wife.

Lacey Ann took after her dad.

She was graced with the kind of consistently colored cream skin that was unmarked by freckles or spots of any kind. She avoided the sun, and with sheets of perfectly cut, blindingly shiny, dark brown hair, the contrast was stunning. But Lacey Ann was unfortunate to inherit her father's large, bulbous nose and learned to avoid the camera at all costs. Years later, as she attended ABT Studio Company to study professional ballet, it was suggested that she have a rhinoplasty in order to secure her career. But the young dancer just couldn't conceive of going through that surgery, and the cracking of her nose bones would give her nightmares.

Lacey Ann's dream of becoming a prima ballerina never wavered. From a very early age, she was fascinated as dancers could sway and spin on their very tiptoes. One day, her mother found her prancing down the street with her toes stuffed in orange juice cans, her little pink tutu flapping in the breeze. Dancing en pointe became her dream, and as she progressed year after year at the Alabama Ballet School, it was obvious that Lacey Ann was destined to dance professionally.

Margot and Mary Grace were bewildered at her determination, giving up school events and cheer practice to perfect her dance combinations at the local studio. Eventually, her parents built a small, mirrored studio above the garage, complete with a Pilates reformer and a state-of-the-art sound system for her classical music. There, Lacey Ann would spend hours stretching, swaying, and spinning across the bleached oak flooring until her every move was perfection. It was her 'happy place', where there was no stress, no boy troubles, no essays to write, and no parents to please. It was just her and the music, and for a moment in time, they were in total sync.

After Margot's graduation luncheon, and a quick spin in her new car, Lacey Ann asked the girls to take her home for practice. She had so much to do, moving to New York in only two weeks. The other girls would spend the summer together without her, and this made her uneasy. The Trifecta had been her life since grade school. They were like sisters; living on the same block for their entire lives; their families as entwined as they were.

The thought of being alone in such a large city, riding the subway and developing street smarts she had never needed, had made her anxious. She kept telling herself that her acceptance into ABT was every dancer's dream, and for that, she was grateful. And Mary Grace kept reminding her that she could be there from D.C. in an hour on the Acela train.

But Lacey Ann's apprehension was making her hungry, something that she had to keep at bay. She could not gain weight, and she had felt pressured to eat at today's luncheon, having been seated next to Margot's mom. She needed to get home, empty her stomach, and practice a routine she had followed all through high school. Controlling her weight was as gratifying as eating a big bowl of mashed potatoes.

Lacey Ann's moods were as erratic as her blood sugar levels. Terrified one minute, euphoric the next. She was excited to explore the city, its magnificent museums, splendid stores, and renowned restaurants. She wanted to shop for groceries at the neighborhood bodegas, Zabar's for special occasions, and wander the narrow streets of bohemian Greenwich Village and the artist haven of SoHo. She dreamed of meandering through the Met, having picnics in Central Park, and people-watching on the Upper East Side. There was just so much to experience and enjoy, and the energy on the streets was high-voltage.

Her parents had reserved a suite at The Stanhope in order to help her settle, obtaining tickets to several Broadway shows while they were there. As a surprise graduation gift, they had hired a decorator to manage the interior design of the co-op they had purchased for her on a beautiful tree-bowered block adjacent to the midtown ballet school. They had arranged a meeting with the school's artistic director while in New York to discuss making a sizable donation in Lacey Ann's honor.

This was immediately accepted, and lunch at the Russian Tea Room was arranged. The Peytons might be from Birmingham, Alabama, but their political prowess was hardly restricted to the Southern section of the United States.

And it just so happened that Patti Peyton's grandfather had been a founding member of the ABT board of trustees.

So, while Patti and Lacey Ann packed the vast Vuitton trunks, stridently checking off the list as they folded and placed each piece into their pressed piles, Paul Peyton spent the afternoons on the golf course. He was avoiding Patti's compulsive need to supervise his packing as well. He had set out several dress shirts and slacks, plus would throw in a tie and sport coat for good measure.

Leaving Lacey Ann in New York, with her teenage tales and gales of laughter, would create a deafening silence in their house, and Paul was dreading the change. He hoped it was all worth it. Many years later, Paul and Patti Peyton would return as the proud parents of their daughter's opening night as prima ballerina of ABT's *Swan Lake*. It was then Paul realized that his delicate yet determined daughter was his life's greatest accomplishment.

Lacey Ann had a stellar career and traveled the world with her company. And, after a disastrous affair with the company's creative director, she swore she would never marry. As she aged off the stage, Lacey Ann stayed with ABT as a teacher, enjoying the excitement and enthusiasm of her young students, while returning home nights to the midtown brownstone she called home.

Over the years, Margot and Mary Grace would visit and loved Lacey Ann's agenda of theater, dance, and symphonies. They ate the best of food but always returned to the Morgan Library for lunch and Bryant Park Cafe for dinner. Bryant Park was inspired by those in Paris and contained the delightful Le Carrousel Magique, which they always rode along with New York's gleeful children. And, because the marvelous New York Library's stacks are housed beneath Bryant Park, the girls always took a look inside the huge stone building flanked by two magnificent lions.

But, as Lacey Ann grew older and her parents older still, she eventually moved back to Birmingham and embraced her Southern roots. She had done it all, fulfilled her dreams, and had a wealth of splendid memories and accomplishments. So she called Margot and asked for help in finding a new home in Birmingham. Margot immediately began raving about her latest move to the most fabulous condominium in town, 777 Wexford, and before Lacey Ann could say 'maybe', Margot had set up an appointment for her to see a unit on three the following week.

Of course, it was perfect, and Lacey Ann loved the open floor plan and the stunning view of Caldwood Park across the street. And, to top it off, the third member of their Trifecta, Mary Grace, was considering selling her home in the suburbs and moving closer to town. Margot was working on her, too.

"Wouldn't it be so fabulous for all three of us to live here?" Margot chirped like a teenager. "Just like old times but better!"

Lacey Ann had to agree. Birmingham had changed so much in her absence, and it would be so comforting to have her two besties nearby while she figured out how to navigate her new life on her own two feet.

Chapter 6
The Application

Margot hurried from her car to the elevator bank where she prayed she wouldn't run into any other residents with her Botoxed, bloated, and bruised face. She had worn her enormous ebony sunglasses and Burberry bucket hat just in case. She was clutching the vacation brochure with white-knuckled anticipation. She was so excited she dropped her keys as she tried to open her front door.

At just that moment, nosy Mrs. Grayson came out her door with a trash bag bulging with God knows what. Unfortunately, her ill-tempered, chocolate-brown Chihuahua, Cruella Nutella, bounded out the door too and was barking furiously and uncontrollably jumping on Margot as she tried to get inside. The commotion caused the gorgeous gentleman across the hall to stick his handsome head out to see what was going on.

"What's wrong with your face?" Mrs. Grayson bellowed down the hall. "There's something wrong with your face."

"I'm fine, thank you," Margot muttered.

"Let me see," said the concerned and eligible bachelor as he gently grabbed Margot's arm. "She looks like a pin cushion. She's all red and swollen. Do you have high blood pressure, my dear?" he inquired.

"No. Please excuse me," Margot pleaded. "I really need to get inside."

With that, the soft-spoken gentleman released Margot's arm, and she hurled herself into the serene safety of her home. The door closed; she took several deep breaths as she learned in yoga, blowing them out slowly as her shoulders began to relax.

The nasty canine Cruella Nutella had scratched her leg, and it was beginning to bleed; she would email a complaint to the HOA Board as dogs were required to be leashed and not run amok through the halls. 'That would teach that offensive old gossip, Mrs. Grayson', she speculated.

After a touch of alcohol and a little Band-Aid was placed on her lacerated leg, Margot poured herself a smooth glass of Sancerre. Lying back on her cream-colored sofa, she took a generous gulp of wine and opened the brochure to read all about the admission process to Rewind Ranch. After that hallway horror show, the idea of escaping to a vacation paradise was sounding better and better.

Margot read the brochure cover to cover. Basically, for a price, you could live in paradise. *That would be a great tagline,'* she thought. But the application request didn't offer much insight into the criteria for admission. There were questions regarding financial status and credit scores. It required a copy of a complete physical examination and passport and a current, full-length photograph. She would have to call the toll-free number and get more information to be sure the girls would be as excited about this as she was becoming.

Margot tried to find more photographs of the paradise online for her sell-job but was unable to find a website. Throwing back another swig of Sancerre, she pulled her cozy, cashmere throw over her legs and settled back for a much-needed nap, dreaming of her new look, new love, and possibly new life.

Hours later, a familiar knock on the door woke Margot from her slumber. Groggily going to answer it, she was greeted by a rowdy, "Hey, gorgeous," coming from her tribe, back from a ladies' lunch. Jewelry jingling and jubilant, the three overserved seniors were checking on their friend's trip to Dr. McDreamy and wanted to throw out some vacation ideas previously presented over their succulent shrimp salads.

Margot listened as attentively as she could before beginning her speech. She wished she had been able to speak to the resort's admissions director first, but after listening to ideas like torturous trail rides through Yosemite and watching bug-infested birds on the Cape, she was rabid to change the direction of the discussion. Gently clearing her throat, Margot began to unfold her discovery at Dr. McDreamy's checkout counter.

The girls were spellbound. It sounded too good to be true. What a marvelous vacation! They wanted to know more as soon as possible, especially about the cost of the three incredible, all-inclusive packages. Margot promised to call the resort that afternoon and report back to the group at coffee in the lobby the very next morning. *'Mission accomplished,'* she thought. More excited and a little less swollen, Margot was the first to secure a seat in the Wexford lobby early the next day. She had enjoyed a lively discussion with Hannah, the ranch admissions director, who answered all of Margot's questions and was sending four full-color admission kits to her that very day. "The season was booking up," she said, "so time was of the essence."

Margot assured Hannah that they would return the completed questionnaires and refundable deposits and schedule their medical exams as soon as possible. She was also ecstatic that Hannah offered to bend the rules for Elli and allow her to pay out her fee in installments.

The girls gathered in the lobby. In the excitement, Margot forgot it was her turn to bring the tray of morning muffins. After much groaning and griping, the subject turned to their upcoming trip. Margot laid out the information gleaned from Hannah. The makeover surgery was requiring one week of their time, with another week or two for healing and physical therapy. Then they must choose whether to stay for two or four more weeks or the platinum package of six months.

Naturally, the cost jumped way up for the latter. Fifty percent of the cost was required immediately, yet refundable with the completed application, depending on their financial statement, physical exam results, and makeover requests. The other fifty percent, after acceptance by the ranch board of trustees, was due on arrival.

Elli groaned.

Margot added, "Hannah will make special arrangements for you, Elli, since we are a group of four potential clients. You have an entire year to pay for your trip in installments, totally interest-free."

"The application packets will be here by tomorrow, so I suggest everyone get on the phone for their physicals and financial arrangements."

With that, the morning muffins were long forgotten, and the ladies were off to wangle their way into a quick clinic visit. The last thing they needed was to miss sending their applications in on time and not be the first in Birmingham to experience the exclusive Rewind Ranch. It sounded like a vacation paradise unmatched by anything they had ever heard of or seen. They each secretly pictured themselves riding bareback on beautiful Palomino horses with their hair blowing in the wind.

Margot finally called Dr. McDreamy to help get them all into his personal primary care doctor for their physical exams after having trouble getting an immediate appointment. And, once the cosmetic physician understood the rush and their eagerness to visit Rewind Ranch, he quickly made arrangements for them all to be seen at the end of the week. He promised their results would be ready to mail on Monday and offered to help with anything else they needed to apply. He didn't mention the ten percent commission he would make if they were accepted.

By Monday, the applications and additions were safely placed in the prepaid envelopes, and Margot herself went to the dreary downtown post office to place them in the mail. She didn't want any mistakes or delays but was horrified at the filthy facility and the mouth-breathing attendant spilling greasy, chopped peanuts, that she was chewing like a slovenly, stoned cow, onto the pristine paper white envelopes she had placed before her.

Margot hoped Hannah didn't think the girls had done that themselves.

Margot had opted for the platinum package: six marvelous, hedonistic months at the resort. *'Why, she might even be crowned Harvest Queen,'* she thought, *'and even stay forever!'* Mary Grace and Lacey Ann applied for a gold membership, and Elli, always one step ahead, talked Hannah into a price break, as well as the payment plan, by offering to work on the resort newsletter, *The Inside Scoop,* while she was there. That way, Elli managed to stay the same amount of time as Mary Grace and Lacey Ann on the gold membership but only paying for the lesser silver.

But it all hinged on the resort board of trustees to vote each of them in.

Waiting for the call from Hannah was torture, but as promised, she rang Margot at the end of the week. Yes, they had all been accepted, and the staff and doctors looked forward to seeing them as soon as they could get there. "When do you think that will be?" Hannah inquired.

Without even asking the other three girls first, Margot couldn't control herself. She practically shouted into her jewel-encrusted iPhone. "We'll be there in a week."

The girls gradually assembled the next morning in the lovely Wexford lobby. Margot looked like the Cheshire cat as she lowered herself into her favorite chair, which faced the elegant expanse of the room. She had worn her new faille caftan and matching Tory tan sandals to the gathering, looking especially festive that morning. It did not go unnoticed. Elli was the first to speak up in her Texas to Southern drawl. After helping herself to Lacey Ann's legendary homemade buttermilk biscuits, Elli broke the ice.

"Going somewhere, Margot?" she quipped.

All eyes turned to Margot. "Not me," she offered with a long, painful pause. "We."

Mary Grace gasped; Lacey Ann squealed; and Elli let out a long, loud, cowgirl whoop. They were on their feet, hugging each other with tears of joy running down their cheeks like they were just crowned Miss Alabama.

"We're due there in a week. Hannah is making all our flight arrangements and will have a car pick us up at the Kahului airport in Maui. Then we'll drive that horrifying Hana Road to the other side of the island."

"If we can survive that, we can do anything," Mary Grace lamented.

The ladies agreed and made a conscious note to bring some extra Dramamine in their Birkin bags. Now the conversation turned to clothes, what surgeries they requested, and how utterly exciting it was to know that in only a few weeks, they would all resemble their fantasy selves and possibly be courted by some exquisitely rich and handsome silver-haired fox.

And, if that didn't happen, they would drown their sorrows drinking Dom Pérignon and eating cracked lobster lounging their splendid-looking selves by the secluded saltwater lagoon. How bad could that be? And that was the downside. The possibility was that they could be married and living in the scenic south of France by Christmas. *'Be still my heart,'* thought Margot.

The flight arrangements couldn't have been better. The ladies were booked in first class all the way. And, to add to the adventure, they had a one-day stopover in San Francisco before embarking on the flight over the Pacific to Maui.

Elli especially loved the Bay Area; its vibrant views took her breath away. She had managed dozens of catalog photo shoots there while living in Manhattan, which allowed her to learn her way around the city, Napa, and Sonoma. It was all so beautiful, full of life and art, and the counter-culture epicenter. People watching on the streets of San Francisco helped her learn what trends were coming in and determined what accessories to pull together for fashion photography shoots.

She also made sure the merchandise was shown to its best advantage and hired the photographers and models requested by the creative director to work on the project. She also helped organize the clothes and supervised the presser and the craft service. It was exhausting but rewarding, and she used her off-time to her advantage.

On weekends, she would go exploring and treat herself to lunch at the French Laundry in Yountville or Chez Panisse in Berkeley. She visited the city's grand museums, spent rainy Saturdays at City Lights Bookstore, or shopped the trendy boutiques in the Mission district and Pacific Heights. She insisted the girls have dinner at the locals' favorite, Bix, hidden away in an alley in the city's Financial District. Later that night, the girls commented that Elli couldn't have chosen better.

Chapter 7
The Journey

After a long flight, connecting in Dallas and arriving at San Francisco airport, the ladies were met by a driver in baggage claim and whisked to a suite at the legendary St. Francis Hotel in Union Square. It was a perfect starting point for Elli's chance to show her favorite city to her favorite friends. Missing rush hour, they were lucky to catch the first cable car clanging up the hill toward Grant Street.

Elli wanted them to see Chinatown first. The entrance was a striking red pagoda surrounded by two massive dragons, and once inside, your world completely changed. Filled with quick-stepping Asians, chatting and clucking in their native Mandarin, there were open markets filled with foods unknown to all four of them. Paper lanterns were strung from houses across the narrow streets, and the smell of smoky incense filled the air. Storefronts were lined with silly souvenirs like toy dragons and straw fans, chopsticks, and coolie hats. Street vendors enticed them with sesame seed chicken on a stick and steamed dumplings.

Elli found her favorite restaurant, the unassuming Red Lantern, a little cafe nestled on the second story of an old office building. Her California Street bus happened to stop across the street from it when she explored the city, and it became her favorite hideaway on rainy Sunday afternoons. Years later, it was featured on television as one of the best, authentic Chinese restaurants in San Francisco. She couldn't believe it was still there, and after a small lunch of hot and sour soup and steamed meat dumplings, the girls continued on their travels to Pacific Heights.

They hopped on the Jackson 3 bus as far as Fillmore Street and browsed the gleaming upscale shops before heading toward the Presidio and all the stately, painted lady Victorian homes along the way. Standing at the top of the Baker Street steps, they marveled at the glorious, international orange Golden Gate Bridge and the columned Palace of Fine Arts below. It was just so breathtaking and beautiful.

Heading back downtown, they window-shopped the fashionable stores off Union Square, spending the majority of time in the Armani store and the Chanel Boutique on Geary. When Elli was here, it used to be hidden away on Maiden Lane off the square. Maiden Lane was named historically after it became the street for local prostitutes to work at the turn of the century before becoming one of the chicest streets in the city.

After a quick but delicious Irish Coffee at Buena Vista, the ladies explored North Beach, stopping into Elli's favorite bookstore where they stocked up on reading material in case the resort was barren of a shop to buy more. The idea was ultimately canceled as Elli reminded them they had to haul them back to the hotel, which was all uphill. They came to realize that the hills in San Francisco meant exactly that.

But the upside was, they concluded, they had worked out enough to cover exercising for at least the next four weeks. They adored the tour but missed seeing Sausalito and Tiburon and many other things as time ran out. They vowed to come back and spend some real time here, going to the touristy wharf, the hip Mission District, and attending the spectacular San Francisco Ballet for Lacey Ann.

Literally throwing their packages into their rooms, they grabbed a cab out front of the hotel to hopefully make their dinner reservation. Driving down the dark and narrow Gold Alley, the ladies wondered if the driver was lost or loco. But, before their nerves got the best of them, he pulled up to an unmarked door and stopped.

Immediately, the door opened, and there appeared a magnificent room full of beautiful people dining on starched white tablecloths lit by tiny ginger jar lamps with white shades. Light jazz played in the background. The ceiling was two stories high with a majestic mezzanine, to which the four dazzled and dumbstruck diners were escorted. The food and ambiance were beyond splendid.

Returning to the hotel, satiated and sleepy, Margot, Lacey Ann, Mary Grace, and Elli barely noticed the luxurious lobby as they headed straight to the brass-encased elevator. Once inside their suite, they said their good nights and proceeded to surrender into a deep, dreamless sleep, preparing for another long flight, and the last leg of their journey to their version of Fantasy Island. They would arrive around noon after being driven up the hairpin curves on the way to Hana. But, at the end of the road, their vacation destination and youth rejuvenation, advertised as 'an over-sixty paradise', would be waiting to entertain, enthrall, and envelop them.

The wake-up call came at a ghastly 4:00 am.

They had hardly had time to throw on the provided, pale pink, plush terry robes before there was a gentle 'knock, knock, knock' on the door and the seductive smell of steaming hot coffee. Lacey Ann directed the cart, complete with a small vase of pale pink peonies, to the center of the room. There the ladies languished over crab and avocado eggs Benedict and freshly toasted sourdough bread. Their flight to Hawaii was at 7:00 am, so they proceeded to the marble-walled bathrooms and showered and dressed. By 5:00 am, they were downstairs, luggage in hand, and climbing into another freshly polished town car for a quick trip to the airport.

They were thrilled that the flight was on time, a miracle in itself these days, and when nestled into their four, first-class seats, they toasted their good luck with a glass of complimentary champagne. Once at cruising altitude, they allowed themselves a peek at the navy blue Pacific Ocean far below, pulled their cashmere travel throws around them, and opened the latest best-sellers to occupy part of their day. After a nap and a small chef salad for lunch, the ladies couldn't withhold their excitement and chatted about their upcoming surgeries like they were going to a casual celebration at the country club.

Finally, the stewardess announced they were landing, and the plane taxied to the Maui air terminal right on time. Once again, a friendly but professional driver met them at baggage claim, and after a presentation of fresh fuchsia orchids, they were on their way to Hana and the vacation of a lifetime. As expected, the road was a series of hairpin turns, not for the faint of heart.

Prepared with Dramamine and a determination to arrive at their destination in style, the white-knuckled ladies freshened their lipstick prior to stepping out of the car and being greeted with earnest enthusiasm by Hannah and her assistant. They were loaded onto the resort's welcome transportation, the Turtle Trolley, driven by a grinning and gregarious gentleman named Rubio. They were whisked away to their bungalow in preparation for an in-depth orientation class, counseling, a surgery pre-op with their team of surgeons, and a spectacular summer vacation they'd surely never ever forget.

Because of a much needed nap, the girls missed dinner, but room service appeared with a before-bedtime snack. They were served from a silver tray filled with assorted rolls and pastries, hot cocoa, and individually baked egg soufflés. When the cart was inconspicuously positioned in the foyer for pick-up, they put on their pajamas and stretched themselves out under the softest down comforters they had ever felt. They needed a good night's sleep, as tomorrow would be busy.

Breakfast at 7:00 am, orientation at 9:00 am, followed by a light lunch. Then at 2:00 pm, each met with their surgical team prior to their 'reengineering', with pre-op beginning the following day. After this conference, there was a lively mixer scheduled for new members and then dinner, which of course they couldn't eat because of their pre-op lab tests. Several days after surgery, they were told, would be a blur as their bodies began the healing process, followed by intense rehab to get them moving again, and enjoying the paradise to which they had come.

The girls had joked that they might not recognize each other after the Friday night mixer, their first chance they would have to be with other guests. "A wild and woolly hoe down, and we're the hoes," they laughed.

It never occurred to them that they might not all make the celebration.

Chapter 8
The Aloha Medical Center

Built into the side of the mountain, surrounded by thick green vegetation sat the stately steel and glass Aloha Medical Center. It was the anchor of the resort and looked down on all the bungalows, beaches, and bistros below. It was protected by a bluff on three sides, so it was impossible to enter any way except through the guarded entrance, which was a narrow steel bridge built over the large, lush ravine. Above the massive teak doors, an architectural detail that was repeated among the burnished steel beams was an imposing sign stating that only medical staff could enter. No visitors were allowed without an approved appointment.

However, as part of the orientation, newcomers were allowed access to the immense lobby, where white coats scurried across the pale gray granite floors. An imposing teak desk was centered on the back wall, managed by two exquisitely beautiful women in crisp white tunics. Behind them was an enormous electronic board that changed almost every second, notating the patients' names and progress throughout the reengineering system. The ladies also noticed a digital gallery of before-and-after photos. "Oh look," said Lacey Ann, "there's a Giselle."

"And a Kim and a Nicole," whispered Elli.

Screen after screen of beautiful faces filled the room, and not just women. They were stunned at the changes into Ben's, Brad's, and Bradley's. And, of course, there were plenty of George Clooney look-a-likes, too.

The technology was almost space age, but it gave the newcomers a sense of security and order; that they would be well looked after while there. The tour guide pointed out that through their database, every surgeon was aware of every patient's progress second by second. Besides the master board, they wore earbuds that were able to communicate verbal commentary to each of them, monitor their patients' vital signs, and announce any patient calls for the nurses on duty assigned to them.

Doctors could also use the high-speed elevators to hasten their trip up to the Healing Center, located on the top floor with expansive ocean views. The sound of rolling waves was piped in as white noise to support the atmosphere of calmness and serenity, and an unlimited supply of morphine and fentanyl was needed for a painless and carefree recovery.

Of course, there were papers to sign, which addressed the usual liability loopholes and cautioned about infections and unforeseen events. All seemed to be in order. There was also a digitized illustration of the results as the doctors saw it so that any misunderstanding could be discussed prior to surgery. Comparing notes and pictures, the Wexford bunch decided the group would all look decidedly different and gorgeous. Leaving the center, they were handed their surgery schedules.

Walking the grounds, from the pool to the spa to the beach and the party huts, all were ready for a quick umbrella drink and a survey of available men at the evening mixer. Interesting that the small party tonight would all be newcomers, something the ladies really appreciated so as to avoid being the ugly stepsisters at the ball.

While Margot, Lacey Ann, and Mary Grace dressed for the party, Elli went to quickly introduce herself at *The Inside Scoop* newspaper office, where a team of editors was proofing tomorrow's edition. They were thrilled to have the help.

As with most newspapers, new writers are first assigned to the obituaries. It never occurred to Elli, or any of the four, that some guests would pass away while here. It made sense, though; they were all old, to begin with, and some stayed six months, while others stayed forever. That thought eased her nervousness, and she thanked the managing editor for trusting her with the back page content, which also included the deadly, black-bordered 'Aloha' obituary column.

Meeting the others by the pool's waterfall, Elli counted a dozen newcomers: nine women and three men. All were well-dressed, and most were overweight. There was an air of tension in the group, but Elli surmised it was in anticipation of the long surgeries ahead of them all and the uncomfortable healing process that followed. For most, it was obvious to see the major things they would want to change about their appearances.

Ed Gleason, an entrepreneur from New Jersey, was terribly overweight, bald on top, and had a huge vertical gap between his discolored front teeth. *'Gastric bypass, veneers, and implants for him,'* Elli thought.

A woman named Gladys from Oklahoma had evidently scorched her skin in the sun in her youth and had more deep wrinkles than a Shar Pei. 'Definitely dermabrasion, facelift, and skin tightening', she guessed.

Elli was about to introduce herself to a frail woman sitting in a lemon-printed lounger when her three besties showed up decked out to death. Elli could hear the distinct, familiar tinkling but couldn't tell if it was the ice in their fruity drinks or their conch shell necklaces purchased at the airport, especially for the trip.

When they got back to their bungalow, Margot discovered that her surgery was at the end of the week, on Friday, with Dr. Michael Staffordshire assigned as her chief surgeon. Trying to be positive, she decided it would give her all week to learn her way around the resort, plus she could have a cheeseburger and fries right this very minute. She figured after her liposuction, they would be taboo so she better enjoy herself while she could. Plus, Margot liked Dr. Staffordshire. He was kind and attentive and quick to answer any questions she had. Mary Grace had Dr. Staffordshire too, with surgery on Thursday.

Dr. Lei would be Lacey's chief surgeon with her procedure that next day. No dinner for her. Lacey Ann had a difficult time understanding Dr. Lei due to his heavy accent. He had come from the Far East only a month prior and was still learning American idioms. He was particularly interested in her being so thin and seemed a bit concerned.

But Lacey Ann assured him her slight weight was nothing new and a requisite for her past career as a dancer. She was so excited to get her nose fixed and some decently sized breasts at this wonderful resort, and she added another request at the last minute. She wanted to add volume to her cheekbones and chin to balance her new face. Dr. Lei quickly added her requests into the computer and assured her as he headed for the door that 'She would rook rovely'.

Elli was a patient of Dr. Meredith Morgan, the only woman surgeon assigned to the four girls, with Elli's surgery scheduled for next

Thursday. Dr. Morgan was new to the resort with a past employment record that included the Mayo Clinic, Johns Hopkins, and the Cosmetic Institute of Geneva. Elli felt she hit pay dirt and immediately bonded with this remarkable woman. She felt completely at ease and could hardly contain her excitement of coming out of this with features similar to the beautiful Margot Robbie.

Not only was she looking forward to her refined facial features, but also getting rid of her faded copper hair and emerging with a thick, blonde mane. After a few presurgery instructions, Dr. Morgan graciously walked Elli to the clinic entrance where she met up with Margot, who was grinning from ear to ear.

She, Mary Grace, and Margot decided to eat out by the pool.

While Elli, Mary Grace, and Margot were chomping on their cheeseburgers, Lacey Ann went to bed exhausted from the day's events. The resort's room service had brought her hot cocoa and sedatives to ensure she would have a restful and relaxing sleep. Obviously, they worked, as her roomies were welcomed with siren-pitched snorting and snoring as they came back inside.

Placing their hotel-provided earbuds into their ears, the three satiated seniors climbed under their three-hundred-thread-count cotton sheets and thought about the adventure that was beginning. It was hard to relax, knowing the changes in the air. But, as the white sounds of the seductive surf began to do their magic, soon they were sound asleep and began dreaming beautiful dreams.

The alarm rang yet again at 6:00 am. That was the signal for Lacey Ann to shower, wash her hair, and remove all jewelry from her body. She dressed in the white caftan and headband given to them at orientation and padded across the suite to the foyer to wait for Rubio in the Turtle Trolley to pick her up for the short journey to the spectacular Aloha Medical Center.

Soon enough, she heard the little bells announcing the trolley's arrival, and climbing in, she was supplied with warm blankets in case she felt chilled in the morning air. Upon arrival, the massive teak doors opened, and the two beautiful receptionists greeted her by name and ushered her to her room in the Pre-Op Center on the fifth floor. Surgery was done on six, they explained, and once it was over, and she was announced stable, she would be wheeled to Recovery on seven before entering a private Healing Suite on eight where she would stay until release.

Everything was so organized and spotless. Everyone was so accommodating and pleasant. The room smelled of fresh eucalyptus, and her bedtime symphony of the surf had been replaced with the soothing sounds of a piano playing Pachelbel's 'Canon in d major'. Although the tiny Birmingham dancer wished her besties' operations were closer to hers, it wasn't long before her eyes became heavy, and she drifted off into another deep sleep, soothed by the slow, soft notes of a beautiful *Baby Grand* playing far, far away.

Lacey Ann woke up with a start. It was almost 8:00 pm. And she quickly realized she was unable to move. Her back was throbbing. Grasping the bed sheet, she found the nurse button and pushed it with all the strength she could muster. A lovely nurse quickly appeared with a comforting smile on her flawless face.

"You woke up, Lacey; welcome back!"

Lacey was temporarily mesmerized by her teeth, which were so splendidly straight and white.

Lacey could only groan.

"Your surgery went great. But, for now, you need to lie very still and rest. No worries. I will give you something for any pain you might feel. Dr. Lei will be here within the hour to speak to you about your recovery."

After an IV was initiated, Lacey Ann once again fell asleep. If Dr. Lei came by, she totally missed him. She was dreaming she was on an island surrounded by people who looked exactly like her; all walking at the water's edge, playing in the surf, and all wearing the very same swimsuit. It was bizarre and unsettling. Evidently, Lacey Ann let out a sharp scream because two enchanting but nervous nurses showed up within seconds.

"Relax, it was just a bad dream," one whispered.

"Now now, dear. Your surgery was wildly successful, and you will be so happy before you know it. Please get some rest."

About that time, the good doctor walked in. "Hello, Lacey," he said, as he sat on the edge of the bed. "How are you feeling?"

Lacey Ann groaned.

"It will get better. And quickly."

Lacey tried to smile but realized her face was still numb, probably from the chin and cheekbone implants they had just put in. And the lip injections, and Botox too. She was dying to touch her nose to feel if the family bump was gone, and it was noticeably smaller. She wondered how much fat they had removed from her small booty, to construct her breasts, but was afraid to ask.

"Get some sleep," Dr. Lei said. "When you awake and are able to sip some broth and use the toilet, we can move you upstairs. The view is much better."

And, with that, he was gone.

Margot, Mary Grace, and Elli had just returned from dinner when a thick white envelope slid under the door of their suite. The luxe-looking note card was embossed with the resort's stylish logo and said, 'Dear Margot, Mary Grace, and Elli, We are happy to report Lacey Ann is awake from her very successful surgery and will be moved to the Recovery area before midnight'. It was signed by the medical center's director of public relations, Kelli Langford, in the most beautiful handwriting they'd ever seen.

'What a lovely gesture', they concluded. They were so thrilled for their friend that they decided an umbrella drink was in order, especially since the next night Elli couldn't partake. So off they went to the Tiki Hut for frozen strawberry daiquiris, which went down so smoothly they could have drunk a dozen.

And, while there, they met a few gentlemen about to have their surgeries too. All the gentlemen were smart, savvy, and entertaining, all CEOs of successful corporations all three girls were familiar with. All needed a little work, too. One was way too pudgy, one desperately needed a chin among other things, and one, a somewhat severely short man named Arnie Katz from New York, had bravely signed up for some serious tibia stretching, a gruesome technique developed in the Far East to add height to their population. His recovery, he was told, would be long, as they can only stretch the bones very slowly for permanent results.

Mary Grace was fascinated and giggled when Arnie mentioned, "The best news is that when I am two inches taller, I will also have a perfectly straight and smaller nose." He was elated. Arnie had a history with horses, and the fact that the ranch also bred and raised award-winning quarter horses was of much interest to him. He planned to stay awhile. It was a win-win situation.

Arnie, like Margot, signed up for the platinum package. He was so pumped to no longer be material for his friends' jokes or to always see the disappointment in his match.com meet-ups as he rose from the table to greet them. They laughed at not recognizing each other the next time they met until Mary Grace jokingly said they needed a code phrase so they would later know to whom they were talking.

Racking their brains, as they slurped down another umbrella drink, they went through dozens of phrases they might use. Fortunately, they eventually agreed on a phrase that was somewhat short, easy to remember, and a definite crowd-pleasing icebreaker. They decided on, 'I have been dying to meet you'.

Elli went quickly to sleep in preparation for her reengineering the next day. Bright and early, red hair damp from a quick shower and scrub, the Turtle Trolley pulled up out front on the dot. With a cheerful 'good morning', the friendly driver helped her on and off they went to the Aloha Medical Center.

On the way, Elli heard the sound of a helicopter that she soon discovered was circling a low-lying building on the cliff's edge. She hadn't remembered seeing that building during the tour and assumed it had something to do with supply storage. Asking the driver if that was correct, he mentioned that he really wasn't sure but had seen medical personnel entering and leaving at night. All his regular pickups and deliveries were from the bungalows to the Med Center and rarely to the physicians' beautiful bunk houses.

Upon arrival, Elli was warmly greeted by the two exquisite nurses and Dr. Morgan herself, who relayed that she liked to greet her patients before surgery in case of any last-minute concerns or questions. Elli really liked the doctor and had complete trust in her, and they chatted like old friends on their way upstairs. Dr. Morgan helped Elli check-in, and then left her with her assigned nurse.

Once out of her white caftan and into her hospital gown, the nurse prepared the IV to relax Elli and then went to alert the anesthesiologist that she was ready to go. A pair of white-clad assistants slowly wheeled her down the hall and into the surgical suite where large luminous lights and soft classical music assaulted her senses. Eight hours later, she found herself in a cool, darkened room unable to move her limbs.

Elli woke to a voice by her bed. It was Dr. Morgan telling her to wake up, the surgery was done, and the doctor swore she was a close second to Margot Robbie. Elli tried to smile, but it was almost impossible. Her face was severely swollen, and her head was wrapped in bandages. Additionally, her torso was well covered with gauze from the breast reduction and targeted liposuction at her waist and thighs. She felt like her face was on fire.

Dr. Morgan gently touched Elli's hand.

"How are you feeling?" she whispered. "Pretty beat up, I bet."

Elli moaned.

"I'll come by in the morning and check on you. Don't be a hero. Use the morphine drip. Stay ahead of the pain. You'll thank me later."

Elli blinked twice to let her know she understood. When the good doctor turned to leave, Elli blinked a third time. Only this time, her eyes stayed closed, and she gently drifted off to sleep.

By Friday, Lacey Ann and Mary Grace were enjoying their adjoining rooms in the Healing Center requested by Kelli Langford, the PR

Director. She knew the girls would heal faster if they had the constant support of their bestie. She also sent them sunflowers to brighten their rooms and their day. Elli was in Recovery and loving the morphine drip, her new best friend.

Margot was slipping on her crisp white caftan for her quick 6:00 am trip in the Turtle Trolley to surgery. When she arrived and was escorted to her room, she thought she saw Arnie being rolled on a gurney down the hall. Once nestled in bed, Dr. Staffordshire entered with a cheerful 'Good morning' and reviewed the digital renderings of her new Charlize Theron self. Her nurse gently knocked and administered the sedative while Dr. Staffordshire went to scrub for surgery. By 7:30 am, Margot was cautiously wheeled to the surgical suite unaware of her surroundings and readied for her transformation to the stunning starlet.

Around 4:00 pm, all three recovering friends were notified that Margot was out of surgery and doing great in Recovery. By Sunday, all four of them would be ensconced in the Healing Center for a week of rest and relaxation while they recovered. They could expect to be released a week after that.

Part of the protocol was the patient's Reveal, a champagne-infused event held in the Healing Center lobby each evening as guests were declared by their physicians to be 'resort ready' and available to mix. Until then, clients were allowed no entrance and no mirrors. It was a casual affair, a come-and-go sort of event, as their 'before and after' photos were illuminated on the walls as they walked the room's runway to Diana Ross' *I'm Coming Out*, a favorite at the resort's discotheque.

The resort stylists pulled designer outfits and professional makeup artists were on tap to complete the job. Their 'after' photos would be published in the week's *Inside Scoop* with a short bio so that interested guests could request a mixer date with anyone they would like to meet.

The girls hoped they could have their Reveal on the same night. It would be such fun preparing for the runway together and actually strutting their stuff like the models they watched at home at Saks. Only for them, a gleaming, full-length mirror was installed on the wall at the end of the runway so they could see themselves. As soon as Lacey Ann was released, they could all schedule their long-awaited Reveal and begin the astonishing adventure of a lifetime.

Chapter 9
Transformations

Two days after the others, Lacey Ann was released from the Healing Center with a small bottle of pills to relieve the pain she still felt in her back. Dr. Lei had explained that because she was so thin, they were forced to extract extra fat from the top of her buttocks, but the wound was healing well. It would just take a little time, and if she was uncomfortable, he would be happy to increase the dosage of her pain pills. Otherwise, she should be thrilled with her results and was sure to be a big hit at her Reveal. She looked pretty much like Keira Knightley's sister.

The four ladies, transformed into their new selves, were escorted to the spa building in fresh white tunics by the dependable Rubio driving the cheerful Turtle Trolley. They were met in the lovely lemon-lacquered lobby by their personal style teams and then were whisked off separately to private rooms filled with mouth-watering designer clothes, shoes, and jewelry, as well as a beauty salon and makeup area filled with every product imaginable.

The team studied the client's file, took photos from every angle, and began to work. After a sensational scalp invigorating wash, their hair was bleached, dyed, highlighted, and low-lighted. Ultimately, it was blown dry and styled. Hair extensions were added as needed, and when done, the hair stylist was replaced by a makeup artist who began by performing a quick dermabrasion and then an extra-strength hydrating mask on their newly familiar faces.

Once the mask was dry and removed, the nail tech began by placing their feet in the pulsating pedicure bowl and applying acrylics to their already waxed hands. They then selected a new but neutral shade of gel polish that would work well with any of the outfits selected for the client. When the nails and toes were done, it was time to break for lunch.

Each of the ladies had hoped this would be their chance to see each other but to no avail. A white-clothed cart was soon wheeled in for each of them carrying little egg-salad sandwiches, with crusts removed, and hot tea that was promised to taste great, fill them up, and not cause their taut new tummies to bloat.

The makeup artists were ready for them, immediately applying a smooth layer of Spackle primer to the four fresh faces. When dry, they sponged concealer under their eyes and then added a perfectly matched foundation all over their faces and necks.

Giving the new color a few minutes to settle and dry, they brushed an iridescent cream blush in the hollow of their cheekbones and finished it with a glowing white highlight above the cheekbones and under the brows. Once their eyes were perfectly prepared with long lashes, they brushed shadow in the creases and lined both top and bottom with a soft crayon. Once smudged, all the ladies had the perfect smoky eyes of their celebrity idols.

The racks of designer duds were wheeled in, and three outfits each were flagged for a fitting. Lacey Ann noticed all her choices were from

Chanel, a great choice since Keira was the face of the legendary brand. Being so thin, her team felt she looked astounding in a long, black, figure-hugging gown accented by one splendid silk camellia. It was a gown very few clients could pull off, but Lacey Ann's boyish, ballerina body was perfect. And the décolleté neckline accentuated her new tastefully added C-cup breasts.

Elli was a different challenge to the fashion stylists. Margot Robbie was her ideal. Immediately keying in on her Texas 'can-do' persona, the team selected three Armani pantsuits, the best choice for draping and fit. They ultimately selected a winter white silk that literally floated when she walked. It was double-breasted, cinched at her now tiny waist and so seductive without a blouse or camisole. With her new blonde hair, she looked smashing.

Mary Grace had the biggest metamorphosis, going from a civil rights lawyer in 'I mean business' ensembles to a very English bohemian type like Sienna Miller. Her hair extensions had been crimped in places, and her natural makeup belied her sassy, sexy self. After going through a dozen outfits, the group dressed her in a midnight blue Valentino velvet midi with embroidered stiletto Jimmy Choo boots, an outfit she was both comfortable in and believable. After practicing her walk with the production team, she opted to change her topaz studs for shoulder-grazing chandeliers that flashed in the light as she stoically and confidently sailed across the room.

Margot, of course, would be elated with her new self, based on Charlize Theron, the dream date of most American men, which was the perfect choice for her. With newly blunt-cut, shoulder-length hair, she would soon feel sexy again with her new face and legs that appeared almost too long to be real. Margot felt sure that the resort would deliver on their promise and was beside herself with anticipation, especially after seeing the before and after photo gallery at the med center.

Gold was the natural color choice for all three fashion selections by the style team; one skinny jumpsuit with a long, net overskirt and two long, body-con dresses. The general consensus was that Margot was a total heart-stopper wearing the jumpsuit, just like in the memorable J'adore perfume commercial. Working with the production team after she was ready, Margot practiced that slow, seductive walk she remembered on television. Finally, after over an hour, she mastered it and loved feeling like a lioness silently stalking its prey.

Five o'clock came none too soon. It was showtime.

The ladies were moved backstage by their handlers at 4:30 pm but were still blindfolded as they received their instructions for the show. They were all assigned a number and knew that prior to their turn, their handler would walk them to the curtain backstage, remove their blindfold, and send them out for the most amazing moment of their lives.

They could hear the crowd gathering as the resort guests read the list of 'Transitions' in their order of appearance and were given small cards where they could check the names of newbies they wished to meet. These were deposited in a large crystal bowl as they left, and Kelli Langford and her staff picked them up and arranged the meetings after reviewing the new 'Transitions' personal files. It was important that the match be a positive and gratifying experience for both parties.

As the crowd gathered around the runway, Kelli Langford took her place at the microphone. The newly reengineered guests were lined up in order of appearance and readied to walk.

The four Wexford ladies were sprinkled among the other ten models; fourteen in all. Margot happened to be number fourteen, a sign she felt was good luck since the bridal gown usually closes a show. Everyone was on edge as they anticipated seeing their new selves in the magnificent mirror leaning against the far wall and steadied themselves not to gasp or shriek when they saw their new selves.

Before they could obsess about it, the music began, and the curtain flew open to a round of rowdy applause. As the production assistants paced the models, each stunning guest strutted their stuff to music, applause, and wolf whistles. It was an exhilarating experience. And, as they approached the mirror, the models slowed down and remembered not to stop per their instructions. But they all burst into a double wide smile at the end of the runway, publicly basking in their new appearance and confidence, and certain that great things were ahead.

It was worth every penny they had.

As the evening Reveal wound down, Kelli Langford gathered the paper ballots checked with black marker. She had spent the evening introducing couples who seemed a good match and thought she saw some sparks as she left them to chat. Margot had already cornered a gentleman from Seattle, a financier with chiseled features and a beautiful smile.

As everyone was dressed by the stylists, it was hard to access the crowd's sense of style and taste. *'That will come,'* she thought. Right now she was putting all her energy in keeping his eyes solely on her and her gold jumpsuit with a neckline that plunged all the way to her waist.

The other three were gathered in a crowd with some of the guys they had met at the pool before their surgeries. They were all talking at once, having a great time at the gathering, and were trying to decide where to grab dinner as the crowd thinned out.

They thought they should celebrate and maybe see if they could get a table at On the Radio, built over the water and known for its brightly illuminated dance floor. It was an eighties disco and played songs by the Bee Gees, Donna Summer, and the Pointer Sisters. It was perfect for them, and they were soon surprised and shocked that they were able to get a table. The girls found Margot, who declined their invitation in hopes Mr. Wonderful would suggest a dinner for two. The girls joined the group out front and piled into the Turtle Trolley.

Mary Grace suddenly noticed that Arnie wasn't at the show. One of the men said he had never come back from the Aloha Medical Center. Remembering the perilous procedure of stretching his legs, Mary Grace realized that it was just too soon for his release and thought nothing of it. She made a mental note to ask Kelli Langford to send a bright bouquet to him tomorrow from all four of the ladies. He was such a sweet man, and she hated to think of him lying there in pain assuming no one cared.

Feeling better, now with a plan to brighten Arnie's tomorrow, Mary Grace made a run to the Turtle Trolley to join all her new and gorgeous friends. She wanted to celebrate everyone's good fortune. Just to think that only a month ago, she was obsessing about her flaws, and today, she was feeling beautiful, something she had really never felt before.

She wondered if everyone felt as euphoric as she did and quickly criticized herself for being so shallow. "Looks are only skin deep," her mom used to say, "it's what's inside that counts." She knew her mom was right, but right this second, being wrong felt so damn good.

Elli knew she would have to make it an early night; not get carried away in her elation. Tomorrow was her first day at work, and she would have to create content for the entire back page of *The Inside Scoop.* This brought her down to earth, as Elli always prided herself in doing a good job; at being creative and innovative yet pragmatic and professional. *'This is going to be quite a challenge,'* she thought. *'How creative can you be with an obituary notice?'*

But she did have a few ideas; information that wasn't being commonly communicated that would be of interest to the guests. She thought some human interest stories on the staff would be interesting; the surgeons and what brought them to Hana, the PR staff and stories they might have of past PR events, the roster of Harvest Queens and where they are now. Elli would have to pitch these slowly as to not appear too pushy but felt she would have a warm reception from the staff and editors as they were always looking for some new slant on old things. 'And yes', Elli laughed to herself, 'there are a whole lot of old things running around this place!'

So off she went to a quick dinner with her newfound friends, with oodles of ideas dancing in her pretty little head.

Chapter 10
The Inside Scoop

The sound of the rapid 'tap, tap, tap' on all the keyboards made Elli feel right at home. She was immediately back in her element. She loved the excitement, the deadlines, and the tension of a newspaper environment. Nothing feels better when you can hold the latest edition in your hands. There is such a feeling of accomplishment and satisfaction. Then you're on to the next one. Besides being a good writer, you have to be flexible, resourceful, tenacious, and curious.

Elli was all of that and more.

The staff met first thing every morning in the marble-tabled conference room, complete with a cappuccino and croissant bar, a far cry from Elli's 'light coffee and a smear' breakfast she was used to grabbing from the neighborhood deli. As she helped herself to some luscious lemon curd, a handsome hunk introduced himself as Shawn, the features editor, who would assign her stories and supervise her work. He was aware of her professional background and was happy to have the help.

As the editor, a young woman who closely resembled Kate Moss called the meeting to order and introduced Elli to the staff. It was almost surreal working in an office filled with beautiful people, all dressed to the nines. The big news of the day seemed to be a major grant given to the resort by a former guest to fund an addition to a building called The Eternity Center, located several miles down the beach.

Elli was assigned to write three obituaries, which always appeared in the Aloha column of the Friday edition. One involved a woman who had become an island resident and recently developed sepsis during another lipo procedure and passed away. It was somewhat of a reality check for Elli, who always considered cosmetic procedures lightly. She was genuinely grateful that she and her besties had suffered no complications in their recent transformations.

She was also assigned the Matched column, which announced recent couplings from the resort's many meetups and mixers. Elli would have to take photos of the happy pairs and interview them on the secrets of their success. It was a way for the resort to gently let other guests know who was off the market and avoid any potential embarrassment when selecting their evening's entertainment and escorts.

She found her first couple lounging out by the pool, lying side by side in the smallest swimwear imaginable. The woman, Joan Hershel, was a now-common Kardashian clone, while her paramour, Peter Wallace, closely resembled George Clooney without the swagger. *'It was interesting,'* Elli thought, *'that no matter what changes about the outside of a person, the internal voice may stay the same.'*

Peter obviously wasn't privy to George's savvy self-confidence. That will come, Elli hoped, or the newfound cougar Kim would move on before poor Peter could say 'Lake Como'. Their poolside table was littered with empty umbrella glasses and the remnants of the jumbo shrimp appetizer that Elli loved so much. Posing them coming out of the pool's pristine, pale aqua water instead, Elli noticed a long slanted scar almost invisibly healing along the base of Joan's berry brown back.

Assuming it was where they inserted the rather large derriere implants, Elli made sure the bright light of the sun didn't capture the temporary flaw on her subject. Graciously turning down their offer to join them in a celebratory cocktail, Elli scooted across the lawn to arrange her second shoot of a couple who wanted to be photographed riding bareback on the beach.

As the sun was moving quickly overhead, Elli arranged to meet the other couple at sunset when the light was much lower and hopefully golden. Shooting portraits during the noon hours was taboo, as the severe shadows caused by the sun being overhead were almost impossible to erase. This accounted for long, long days in Elli's previous art director world, as everyone needed to be up and ready at sunrise and fresh and motivated at sunset. But it was a wonderful, exhilarating, and exciting career full of fun people and endless travel, and she gratefully enjoyed every minute of it. It was really the best years of her life.

Elli took a break in her day to grab a quick sandwich at Poi George, choosing an Ahi Tuna BLT. The food at this resort was beyond delicious, and it was all she could do to resist the Truffle Fries on the menu. She had to be careful about her newly celebrated weight loss. Gaining it back would be a travesty, one she didn't want and, God knows, couldn't afford. The thought of this brought her down to earth, and she carefully removed the soft, sourdough bread from the second half of her sandwich.

Passing on her pasta salad, Elli took a large swig of her diet raspberry iced tea and headed back to the office to write her first story. The soothing sound of keys typing away hit Elli's ears the minute she entered the office. She hadn't realized how much she missed the challenge and camaraderie of an office setting, and she marveled at how happy she was working again. Nestling into her cubicle, she scanned her photos of Joan and Peter and began to think of an opening line that would grab the readers' attention.

She decided that since they were both successful investment bankers, she would slant her article to their feeling like coming here was the best investment they had ever made. She ended it with a sexy statement from Peter that 'the Dow wasn't the only thing that was up'.

Checking with Shawn that maybe she had gone too far, Elli was delighted that he thought it was great and something their readers would get a big kick out of. "We need more of this, Elli," he said. "We are in the entertainment business too. We need to be sure everyone is enjoying themselves here at the ranch."

'One down,' she thought.

After confirming with the riding stables that two, very complacent and calm ponies would be ready on the beach at 6:00 pm, Elli scanned the fact sheets describing the detailed obituaries for the week. One was a gentleman from Georgia who had been there for months and had returned to the Aloha Medical Center for additional work to slim down his 'love handles'. He was well-liked, obviously, and had hooked up recently with a woman newly transformed from Connecticut.

That, Elli assumed, was the catalyst for him wanting to look a tiny bit better. His doctor, a renowned surgeon newly recruited from overseas, was quoted as saying how the gentleman's surgery had gone very, very well, but unfortunately, his heart had given out during his recovery. His remains were cremated at The Eternity Center and shipped home to a daughter who lived outside of Atlanta.

The other obits were for two women who had just recently arrived for massive liposuction and gastric bypass surgeries. Upon arrival, after passing their pre-op with flying colors, it seems they somehow contracted sepsis, and passed away from infection. The Aloha Medical Center staff was devastated, and Elli wanted to end her story with a quote about the women's personal lives, something that would humanize the tragedy. Unfortunately, both had no family, so Elli was forced to try to get quotes from the women's surgeon, Dr. Huang Lei, and one from public relations director, Kelli Langford.

Kelli proved to be an interesting twist on the resort's operations. Having no luck contacting the surgeon, who was 'always prepping for, or performing, surgery', Kelli explained the resort's policy on cremation disposal when no family exists and the remains were not claimed. They contracted with the Farewell Wave Society who picked up the canisters monthly and sailed a large wooden schooner out into the ocean at night for a solemn disposal ceremony. It was nicknamed The Crystal Ship, based on lyrics by Jim Morrison of the Doors.

Seems the lead singer also wrote poetry, this particular song was known for its halting beat and haunting lyrics, Morrison pens his love for a former flame and promises she will never be forgotten. It seemed a fitting name for the ship and a somber song for the situation at hand. Ranch guests were welcome on the short seafaring voyage to pay tribute and salute the deceased.

While some actually knew them, others just welcomed a midnight sail and the opportunity to mingle at another resort gathering, no matter how grim the circumstances. Curiously, the group seemed to revel in the ominous and eerie vocals across the still sheets of seawater that surrounded the slowly sailing ship as it slipped silently into the night.

Elli made a mental note to attend one of these sailings in the near future. The entire process interested her, and it seemed to be a great resource for a very interesting news article. So Kelli assured her she would email her the details of the next disposal and save her a seat. Glancing at her watch, Elli realized she had spent way too long on her article and needed to head for the beach to photograph the other couple for her column. The sun was setting, the light a perfect golden, yet she couldn't shake the haunting sound of Jim Morrison and those lithesome lyrics from her mind.

The beach shoot was magical. Two eighty-year-young guests (so she was told) looked fit and vibrant and madly in love. He, a recent widower from San Francisco, and she a long-time divorcee from Miami seemed to really hit it off. It was a match made in 'paradise'; they laughed to themselves; and it gave Elli a glimmer of hope for her future and that of her three friends.

The couple was busy making plans for her to move into his St. Regis apartment downtown and also supervise redecorating the Mendocino house. It is there that they will keep their horses, a wedding present for each of them. It was only fitting that their *Inside Scoop* photo be one of them riding together into the sunset.

Elli couldn't wait to tell the others about her day.

As she returned to the office and chose a beautiful shot of the two cantering across the sand, Elli quickly wrote her story about the lucky-in-love twosome and submitted it and her photograph to Shawn's lovely assistant for his approval. With her day's work done, Elli organized her desk for tomorrow and scurried over to the Blow Bar for a quick wash before returning to her suite to get dressed for her first match. She hoped it was a good one, as she scheduled it as a self-love gift for braving her surgeries and doing something so wildly out of her comfort zone.

Lacey Ann had a date tonight too, so they shared the usual blind date anxiety they experienced as teenagers and gave each other much-needed and overused pep talks about how lucky these guys were to meet them.

Margot was going to the disco again with Mr. Wonderful, a meetup that seemed to be going quite well.

Mary Grace opted to stay home that evening, as the night before she was out for all hours with the group from the pool, minus Arnie. Mary Grace hoped the flowers had been delivered so he knew they were thinking of him and wishing him a speedy recovery. She had begun to feel that the pool group was her only 'real' connection so far, probably because they had all met and accepted each other as they were; warts and all. Mary Grace was beginning to wonder if finding true love was really possible here, where everyone you looked at was nothing short of pure perfection.

Chapter 11
Another Day in Paradise

Phil Collins had taken over her brain much like Barry White had done to Ally McBeal.

Lacey Ann kept mouthing the words as she tried to sit up in bed. 'Oh, think twice, 'cause it's another day for you; You and me in paradise'. Her head was pounding, but worse was the searing pain coming from the base of her spine. She quickly reached for her almost empty bottle of pain pills.

She knew all that dancing was not the thing to do last night, but between her adorable date, the watermelon margaritas, and the pain pill she took right before she went out, she spent the evening pretty much wasted. She prayed she didn't embarrass herself in front of Beau, her first selected, Southern gentleman straight from the symphony in Charlotte, North Carolina. He played the cello, an instrument Lacey Ann adored; its melancholy vibrations always calmed her down.

She had tried to learn to play the cello as a child, intrigued not only by its mellow melodic tones but by the beauty of its highly varnished wood and voluptuous, almost sensual curves. She just didn't have the focus needed to play it well, as her eyes always wandered to what was also happening on stage. Her love of dance won out, and Lacey Ann couldn't live without the absolute freedom she felt when her movement and the music melded together. She felt compelled to follow her dream en pointe.

But last night was a different animal. It wasn't a proper plie she was doing but disco dancing at On the Radio with her date. He was a great partner and brilliantly led Lacey Ann through all the steps made famous by John Travolta. His joy on the dance floor was contagious, and Lacey Ann found herself throwing her head back in glee, spinning and swaying to the music. He couldn't believe he had lucked out with someone as proficient as him and was thrilled she also loved classical music, dancing with abandon, and quiet evenings by a crackling fire just as he did.

They marveled at the resort's ability to match people, and both had silent wishes that this was only the beginning. Plus, they both had more matches to come if they wished and wondered where the other one stood on the subject. After a few more outings, with similar success, Beau decided he would bring it up over a romantic dinner. Lacey Ann could be the girl he dreamed of, and he wasn't about to let her slip away. Not yet, anyway.

A sharp pain brought Lacey Ann back to reality as she turned the heating pad up higher to ease her lower back. She considered calling her doctor, but the language barrier with Dr. Lei made her uncomfortable, so she decided just to refill her meds and maybe schedule a soothing massage at the Spa House that afternoon.

Not wanting to dress, she called room service and was delighted that in just ten minutes, her hot pot of Earl Grey and almond croissant were being rolled into her room with the morning's *Inside Scoop* newspaper and a clear crystal vase of pretty pink peonies. The tea was wonderfully calming, and she immediately felt better; well enough to fall into a deep sleep where she dreamed of her limber limbs leaping across a shining stage lit by a thousand tiny lights that shone like stars in the night sky.

Her performance ended when Elli burst into the room clutching today's newsletter. "Did you see my back page?" she breathlessly asked. Momentarily confused and half-asleep, Lacey Ann slurred an answer that sounded like she was on a weekend bender. Elli sat on the side of the bed and glanced at the empty pill bottle.

"My back is killing me," Lacey Ann muttered. "Too much dancing last night, I'm afraid." Rolling onto her stomach, Elli glanced at her friend's badly bruised back and noticed the tiny stitched scar at the base of Lacey Ann's spine. "If you're not better at lunchtime, I am going to call your doctor," Elli announced.

There was something unsettling about Lacey's little scar, but in a rush to get back to the office, she couldn't quite place it. But then she reminded herself that surgery was surgery, no matter where you had it done, and instantaneous healing was a pipe dream. No matter how many mixers, matches, or massages you were showered with, your body has been traumatized, and no diversion or umbrella drink could change that.

When she rounded the corner to her cubicle, Elli's eye was caught by the flash of a dozen yellow roses flanking her computer. They were from Scott, her match from the previous night. She slipped the card into her pocket to show the girls when they met for lunch at noon.

Margot's many magnificent matches would probably dominate the conversation anyway.

It was one thing to be pursued, but with all her matches being just about perfect, it was creating somewhat of a problem. She realized she owed none of the gentleman anything, but it had never been her thing to date several men at one time. She was a serial monogamist and that never really occurred to her when she signed up for so many matches. The girls told her to relax and enjoy it, but it was hard for her, always juggling invitations and trying to focus on her true feelings. That seemed to be the downside of perfection; when everything was so right, how can anything be so wrong?

Tonight, she was once again going out with Arthur, the man from Seattle she met the night of her big Reveal. They had been seeing each other several times a week, usually luncheons or walks on the beach. He wasn't a big party animal, and despite the fact that he looked like Rock Hudson, the financier kept a pretty low profile in the evenings. The bright side of that is they had long, lovely conversations, and Margot felt he was a truly kind soul, not one of these lady killers sauntering around shirtless and smirking. It was so true, 'money can't buy class', she recounted, something her mother drilled into her head as she went off to college.

Arthur had been divorced for almost a decade and seemed to put most of his energy into his job. He had two grown daughters and a half-dozen grandchildren whom he adored. But the center of his life was Pippa, his golden retriever and companion for the past seven years. Margot was surprised at herself for being attracted to someone so 'normal' and not one of the oligarchs trying to catch her eye at every turn.

At some point, the girls were going to have to take her problem seriously and give her some well-needed advice. Being so popular was a great deal of fun, but not totally satisfying. The annual Harvest Queen contest was coming up in a month or so, and Margot was no fool. She knew she had to maintain her high profile and a slew of suitors to garner votes. So, for that, she needed to lighten up and enjoy the attention.

Running into Marco, one of her favorite matches, she quickly exchanged air kisses and a hug. She was late to Poi George, and she knew Elli would have to get back to work. So off she went to join her besties, *'Have a Bloody Mary and today,'* she thought, *'a big old greasy hamburger.'*

Mary Grace arrived first, followed by Margot, and then ten minutes later, Elli hurried in.

"I've been trying to speak with Lacey Ann's doctor," she said in frustration. "You can hardly understand him, and all he wants to do is increase her pain meds. She just doesn't look well, and her back is hurting again."

Margot almost rolled her eyes. "She was told they had to lipo out of her butt because she's so ridiculously thin to make her new boobs. She didn't want silicone, remember?"

"Right, right. I'm just worried about her. I want her to have a good time like the rest of us. Speaking of…"

Elli launched into a blow-by-blow of her date last night ending with the arrival of her bright yellow rose of Texas bouquet. Her match had actually been from Oklahoma, a rancher by the name of Scott Markam. They joked about the annual Texas–OU football game weekend in Dallas and how as teenagers they were deep into the downtown traffic, drinking beer with their buddies, and praying their parents would never find out. They both loved the state fair and tried to make it back every October to eat their Fletcher's Corny Dog and taste all the bizarre fried food showcased that year.

Scott even knew the owner of Boris, the gigantic thousand-pound hog who was on display every year, and with whom Elli always had her photo taken. It was a great match, and Scott even seemed intrigued by Elli's design background and her career in fashion and publishing. She in turn loved the outdoors but was so grateful that the only outward sign that he was a cowboy in the way he put himself together was his Lucchese alligator boots. They cost as much as her car.

Scott went to SMU where he earned his master's degree, but after working as a stockbroker for several years in downtown Dallas, he said he was tired of dealing with the pressures of the financial world and missed being outdoors. He grew up on a farm in Enid and was lucky to get a football scholarship to Southern Methodist, as his parents could never afford such a tony school. And, although he did really well financially, Scott never forgot where he came from. He was not only cute, kind, and intelligent, but generous as well. Elli liked him immediately.

He had recently bought a cottage on Cape Cod after visiting some old college buddies and was learning to sail. He had never been around water, growing up on a dusty Oklahoma farm, and was enamored with the beach and the ocean and all the wildlife he had never seen before. Seals and whales leaped from the waters around him, and birds he never knew existed, like the huge osprey, were plentiful.

And, of course, Scott delighted in the huge, freshly caught lobsters he could purchase straight from the schooners at dusk as they unloaded their day's bounty. He planned to spend the summers up there, deep sea fishing and sailing his new boat to nearby Nantucket, another new place that had sparked his interest. He had joined a sailing club, along with his old frat brothers, whose membership came from all across the world. He was beginning to forge new friendships and learn of ecological organizations really needing financial help to keep these magnificent creatures safe, something he took a real interest in.

Elli was enraptured too. She loved his enthusiasm and sense of adventure, as well as his sensitivity to wanting to support these things that brought him such joy. She had directed several photo shoots on the Cape and had fallen in love with it too. As their first date progressed, Mr. Scott Markam was beginning to really interest her, and by the time they said their goodbyes, she couldn't wait to see him again.

Mary Grace and Margot listened intently to Elli's news. She was such a no-nonsense type of girl that they both took her infatuation seriously. Margot, on the other hand, had always been a man-magnet and a touch of a drama queen, so her midday whining about pressure from her bevy of beautiful bachelors fell on deaf ears.

Mary Grace, who was slowly sipping on her bowl of chilled gazpacho, was unusually quiet during the dating discussion. She had yet to go on her first match, who appeared to be a very successful civil engineer from Nashville. Silver-haired with chiseled features, the handsome, high-profile hunk had been widowed ten years prior and owned a palatial home in the star-studded suburb of Belle Meade. He actually lived next to Grammy-winning country music stars and socialized with them and other mega country stars all the time.

It was all a bit intimidating to Mary Grace, who shied away from such things and had devoted her life to helping the under served. She really couldn't understand why they had matched her with him, this Mr. Vincent Blalock of Belle Meade, the extravagant epicenter of the country music scene. Of course, she didn't know that for sure but wondered what on earth she would have in common with him and his famous neighbors.

Of course, Margot and Elli thought he sounded great; they almost wished they had been matched with him and tried to talk Mary Grace into calling him back and setting something up. They had seen him in the clubs surrounded by the resort's finest female population, so they were afraid if Mary Grace didn't make her move she would blow it.

Of course, there would be others, but the ladies learned from guests who had been there a while that your first match was the best. It was the one that garnered the highest compatibility score and had the best chance of being something long-lasting. As the dates and additional matches came later and later, the chances became slimmer. Kelli Langford had explained all this in one of the resort's relationship classes held in the dining room during off hours. The girls hadn't really been there long enough to take advantage of the long list of classes and workshops that accompanied the roster of mixers, tours, and dances.

And let's be honest, when given a choice between a magnificent masquerade ball and a workshop, which one would you pick? They vowed to review the resort catalog of events after dinner so they could make more productive decisions, and Mary Grace promised she would contact Vincent this afternoon and see if he was up for a short, sunset stroll on the soft sands of Hana.

Elli took half her sandwich back to the office to munch on later. She swore it was the best chicken salad she had ever tasted. It would be a miracle if she didn't gain ten pounds just eating in this place. Making a mental note to cool it, she reached for the daily reports which contained the fact sheets for the articles she needed to craft for *The Inside Scoop.*

She figured she would tackle the bios of the newest personnel first and then research and write a feature on the upcoming Harvest Queen contest. It would be a much bigger opportunity to showcase her creativity and explore another facet of this fabulous place.

There were two new employees this week. One, an attractive surgeon from Beijing, who had been educated in London and had done her residency and first few years of practice at Manhattan General. The other was a James-Beard-award-winning chef from Chicago, who had been hired to run the newest resort vegetarian eatery, The Meet Market, a vegan-inspired meatless charcuterie complete with black-and-white-tile floors, ornate iron-based tables, and frilly French wire chandeliers. Elli was amazed at the interesting people the resort employed, all the best in their professional fields. It would be fun to know more about these accomplished associates.

She briefly wondered how the parent company could afford to hire so many talented professionals until she quickly remembered the cost of this place. Since she was working off over half of her fees, Elli had a distorted view of the price people were paying for perfection. Both newcomers had professional photographs attached to their fact sheets, and both looked as if they themselves had spent a few weeks in the Aloha Medical Center prior to their work assignments.

Dr. Wu was gorgeous. Her skin was flawless, her features refined, and her hair like sheets of glossy black glass. The chef was pretty much a body double for Bradley Cooper, and Elli silently wondered if he was on the match program in his spare time.

"Probably not," she whispered to herself. "What a waste."

But then those bright yellow roses caught her eye yet again, and visions of Scott clouded her consciousness. He really was a doll, and she hoped he would ask to see her again soon. Lord knows who else he had been matched with, and although she had a date for a drink after work, she wondered how she would feel if she ran into him out with yet another beauty. It was all part of the process, she knew, but somehow, it sounded so much better reading about it than actually experiencing it.

Plus, it was one freaking date. She had to get a grip and stop getting ahead of herself. She knew this match thing was getting in her head, and that was a bad place to be. It is supposed to be a vacation, not a competition. If only it felt like that.

Before she left, an obit fact sheet crossed her desk, and she immediately filed it in the folder for this Friday's back page. So far it was the only one and that made Elli feel a bit of relief. She would much rather concentrate on the Harvest Queen contest and happier thoughts. It never occurred to her that death would even be thought at such a magical place. It was such a dichotomy with the tinkle of ice in the delicious drinks and the purr of cocktail chatter coming from a crowd too beautiful to describe.

The scenery was a picture postcard, too, no matter where you gazed, and the weather was as perfect as it gets. The commonly known Hawaiian rains actually fell on the island's other side, divided by a massive mountain of volcanic rock, and provided much-needed water to the many acres of manicured golf courses that drew thousands of tourists annually to its widely known resorts. This was a smaller and more cultured corner of the island. Plus it raised those magnificent animals.

Few of the world's population were even aware of the island's more deserted east side, allowing secluded and substantially more expensive destinations to those wanting to avoid the masses. And the highly publicized road to Hana added to the aura of seclusion and mystique.

Not for the faint of heart, its twists and turns along the mountain's edge were enough to deter anyone from venturing to the other side. Most timid travelers satisfied themselves with the 'I survived the road to Hana' T-shirts available for purchase in all the local gift shops along with the prized pukka shell necklaces they grabbed by the handfuls like cocaine-laced looters.

It took several seconds for Elli to realize her cell phone was ringing, flashing Mary Grace's name as it rang. She tried to silence it, but it was buried under stacks of papers on her desk and worried that the staff would not only be annoyed at the loud intrusion but roll their eyes when they heard Lionel Ritchie wailing his 1983 lyrics.

Mary Grace had finally mustered up the nerve to call Vincent, whom she now referred to as Vince, and made a date for late that afternoon. He sounded happy she had called, which eased her apprehension at extending herself. His easy conversation gave her hope that maybe they would actually connect. She couldn't wait to report to Elli that she had made the call. But Elli was frying bigger fish.

Entering the vast Aloha Medical Center lobby, Elli was once again awed by the exclusive environment of pristine floors and digitized walls showing incredible surgical transformations. The soft smell of eucalyptus was so refreshing, and the beautiful hostesses in their crisp white tunics were warm and welcoming. As she approached the desk, she realized she only knew Arnie's first name, so she was hopeful that she could get some information on his condition and when he would be joining the rest of them in the resort festivities.

After a few phone calls and a search on the computer listing of current Aloha Medical Center guests, the agent finally found his name: Arnold Jacob Katz III. He was now in the Skilled Nursing unit, as the bone stretching was a slow and painful process. He was doing very well, she mentioned, but there were absolutely no visitors allowed in the Skilled Nursing section.

Elli asked if she could leave a message or a note for him, and the agent graciously took it all down and promised to deliver it to Mr. Katz that afternoon. Elli even added a cheerful and colorful Aloha Balloon Bouquet to her request and charged it all to their bungalow.

Feeling a tiny bit better about Arnie's situation, Elli returned to her suite and reassured Mary Grace that Arnie was doing fine. They were all concerned, of course, as to what was going on.

But Mary Grace was now making an appointment for a professional makeup job before her sunset soiree. She knew the difference between an air-brushed application of her foundation versus doing it herself was shocking. Now she knew why all those celebrities always looked flawless, and tonight so would she. She might even invest in that white linen and lace midi-dress she saw in the shops yesterday.

Walking in that dreamy dress blowing softly in the sea breeze with a handsome hunk was what she imagined for tonight's rendezvous. And, with that in mind, she headed for the shops with the decision to purchase that designer dress, get her makeup done, and be waiting down at the beach with a bottle of cold champagne in hand for this supposedly perfect Mr. Vincent Blalock of Belle Meade, Tennessee.

Chapter 12
Arnold Jacob Katz III

All his life, Arnold Jacob Katz III was teased relentlessly for being short.

Born the only son of a Jewish immigrant, his parents entered this country via Ellis Island during the outbreak of World War II. Settling in Manhattan's Upper West Side like so many Jewish immigrants, young Arnold was a latchkey kid while his mother scrubbed floors and his father cleaned out horse stalls that housed the horses that pulled the tourist-filled carriages at Central Park.

Arnold spent his afternoons inside their one-room walk-up reading books that he chose on Saturdays at the exquisite lion-flanked library on Fifth Avenue. Playing outside was too treacherous for him; the street bullies beat him up and taunted and teased him about his small stature and large nose. It didn't help that he could hardly speak English.

The senior Arnold Katz was fortunate to find work with the stables. He was raised on a Bavarian farm where his father owned three beautiful stallions. A jockey by trade, he was in demand for his services and amassed a small fortune during his reign on the racetrack. This allowed young Arnold to attend well-respected boarding schools and was focused on someday earning a degree in Equine Studies at an agricultural university before working at Poland's Lublin Racetrack.

But the war took its toll on racing in Poland. The Germans stole the best horses and breeding stock from private owners and put them out of business. Arnold senior, realizing that his family would ultimately be in danger, quickly prepared his family to relocate to the United States, knowing it would mean leaving everything they owned behind.

Young Arnie, as his son was called, inherited his father's love of horses. He actually loved most animals and decided to dedicate his life to taking care of them. After earning his undergraduate degree at NYU, Arnie was accepted and earned his doctor of veterinary medicine degree from Cornell, based in Ithaca, New York. While there, he met a gregarious and gorgeous girl named Melinda Marks and fell madly in love.

Melinda was from a farm in Ohio and shared his passion for animals, international cooking, and the importance of family. They married soon after graduation and moved to an apartment in Queens Village, New York, where she could pursue her dreams in Manhattan and he could conveniently ride the Long Island Railroad to Belmont Park. It also placed them close to Arnie's parents, who adored their new daughter-in-law and hosted them for brunch every Sunday. It was on those days that Arnie's mother taught Melinda to cook his favorite dishes.

One Sunday, as Melinda was stirring the matzo ball soup, Arnie's favorite, she fell to the kitchen floor dead from an aneurysm. It was a shock to everyone and left Arnie devastated. He threw himself into his work, moved to Basking Ridge, New Jersey, and eventually began to raise race horses. With his vast knowledge of the animals' physiology, temperament, and training techniques, he was enormously successful and made millions, the latter being a magnet for the surrounding matrons.

After two disastrous marriages, Arnie gave up on women and focused on his beloved horses, 'My only stable relationship', he would joke. It was years later as he was leaving his doctor's office, after finally correcting his deviated septum, that Arnie Jacob Katz III picked up a brochure on the remarkable Rewind Ranch.

With money to burn and a flaming desire to be courted for more than his money, Arnie applied and was accepted. As he settled into his first-class seat headed to Hana, he gazed out the window at the big, billowing clouds below, and wondered what had ever possessed him to do this. Once he arrived, Arnie made guy friends with ease and felt like he was really going to enjoy this much-needed vacation.

Despite the enormous cost, the property was pristine, the food delicious, the women beautiful, and the activities offered right up his alley. He couldn't wait to saddle up at the beach, and boogie down at the 80s disco On the Radio. The only drawback was his transformation, something that sounded like a great idea but now the reality was setting in. He wondered since he had lived with his large nose for seventy years, why it bothered him now. And the thought of stretching his leg bones gave him the creeps, although it would be fantastic to be two inches taller, the maximum expansion one could expect from the terrifying treatment.

They told him today that he had gained an inch in each tibia, the main bone from the knee on down. Next week, they would address his femurs and try to gain another inch there. Soon he would be out at the pool with his new friends, 5'9" tall and with the most handsome nose in town. Arnie also opted for some stomach and love handle lipo and implants that looked like an instant six-pack. In the meantime, he lived in a morphine haze that would make Jimmy Hendrix proud.

Trying to get comfortable, he gazed at the bright balloon bouquet sent to him by the sensitive and smart Southern girls he met a few weeks prior by the pool. They were all gorgeous, but there was one he would like to see in the future, a horse lover and lawyer named Mary Grace. Arnie hoped she was still around and available when he was finally released by his doctor. He just had an instinct about her, much like he did about his high-stakes winning race horses.

About that time, Dr. Lei came in to check his recovery and was particularly interested in his lingering lipo pain, which seemed to be getting worse, not better. He was purple with bruising and had developed a low-grade fever. "Not worried," Dr. Lei quipped, "you're fine."

And so with that, Dr. Lei injected Arnie's infusion line with another syringe of a clear liquid that surely would relieve his aches and pains. This time, it was fentanyl. And, as he tingled from head to toe, Arnie began to feel the weightless haze course through his body, as the pain subsided and the room blurred to black, and Arnie floated above his bed and heard Jimmy sensually sing into his loudly ringing ears, 'Excuse me, while I kiss the sky'.

It was almost a day later when Arnie finally emerged from his deep, dope-induced sleep, compliments of Dr. Lei.

It was that very day that the surgical rounds informed him that Dr. Lei had ordered another blood test and found an unusual bacteria in Arnie's system. The good news was that they were able to identify it and match it with a different antibiotic that they would begin injecting that afternoon, and Arnie's back pain should quickly subside. They were also pleased with the elasticity of his femurs, which had elongated a quarter of an inch already, and Arnie should be good to go to rehab by the end of the next week. It was great news, and Arnie celebrated with a small dish of his favorite Rocky Road ice cream, but not too much, as he wanted to be as tall and trim as possible when he joined the feverish festivities outside.

About that time, Arnie's nurse appeared with another bag of clear liquid, headed for the stainless stand next to his bed. "Time for a little nap, Mr. Katz," she announced.

And, with that, the now slightly taller Arnie Katz felt his eyes go as heavy as the big belly he used to carry around and close. *'Back to dreamland,'* he thought, as time itself drifted away, and Arnie Katz was once again in a purple world all his own.

Chapter 13
Flaming Matches

Mary Grace floated from the designer dress shop on cloud nine. She felt, and looked, like a million bucks. Her hair was pulled back in a perfect 'messy bun', a sure shield against the ocean's billowing breeze. Her makeup was flawless, and her perfectly positioned false eyelashes made her eyes look enormous. Her white linen dress looked custom-made for her slim frame and complimented with her favorite find, a white leather Tory Burch Miller sandal. She looked like an angel, the salespeople said, and if this eager bachelor from Belle Meade didn't think so, he definitely needed additional eye surgery.

Her appearance belied her anxiety.

Mary Grace was trying to be positive but still couldn't understand what they would have in common. He was just too much; too handsome, too rich, too powerfully connected. Can you even imagine hanging out with celebrities? What on earth would Mary Grace have to talk about at their neighborhood cookouts?

She was totally intimidated but tried to remind herself she paid a lot of money to trust these professional matchmakers. She hadn't had any luck so far, and how bad could this be? She needed to learn to live in the moment and not write a story on every encounter she would have here. *'Let things develop naturally,'* she thought to herself, *'much unlike the island's clientele.'* Herself included.

Meanwhile, Vincent Blalock had spent the day by the pool, listening to the latest country music wannabe Kitty Rydell. Kitty was a twenty-three-year-old Miranda Lambert look-alike but was a little rough around the edges. She was a country girl, raised in the trailer-home people always imagined, but had a voice that could blow a double-wide across the county.

Kitty had been invited to their neighborhood monthly cookout to entertain the casual group and had cornered him at the grill, at which he was flipping burgers for the crowd. She had assumed he was in the record business like so many of his neighbors as she pressed her newest CD into his hands. She also tried to press more than that, but Vince quickly turned away, and Kitty barely missed scorching herself on the grill. Seeing her handbag was filled with the CDs, he promised to listen to it and pass it on to one of his producer neighbors.

But Vince's mind was not on Kitty Rydell. It was that down-to-earth, compassionate Mary Grace, who had captured his imagination. Shy and soft-spoken, she didn't seem as rabid as some of the women he had been matched with. He liked her from that first call, which was unusual for him.

Vince was old-fashioned that way. He was a man's man yet was passionate about the world's poorer communities. His mother had worked tirelessly to help the homeless in his native Chicago, and he spent many a Sunday serving food in the local shelters. She wanted him to be grateful for the life he had been born into, one of prosperity and privilege. Later in life, after earning his master's in civil engineering at

MIT in Cambridge, Vince worked tirelessly to get ahead but also remained generous to the underserved in Nashville, where he resided. He had even financed the city's new homeless facility, which bore his name.

Yes, Mary Grace sounded like his type; and he could well imagine her as a life partner in helping others. Her empathy excited him, and he imagined them sitting outside on the deck, watching the sunset over the beautiful Blue Ridge Mountains in the evening.

The resort was hosting a limbo party that evening, so Vince thought that they would have a drink there after meeting on the beach. It would be casual and fun, and then he had made reservations for a delicious dinner at the resort's finest restaurant. He wanted to make a good impression but not be too stuffy. The quiet dinner would give them a chance to actually talk and learn more about each other without the boisterous bellows of the resort's planned events.

There, the booze flowed freely, and the crowd's compromised comfort zone was always tempting them to have 'just one more' as they tried to impress and watched the single ladies wantonly want an introduction and then a romantic date. Sometimes, it was awkward at best, with all those eyes on you, waiting for the right response before you could politely step away.

Of course, Vince knew he was there for the same reason. He wanted to find that special person to complete his wonderful life. He just wasn't going to settle, regardless of the cost. He was taught 'quality over quantity', and it had always served him well. With that thought, he pulled on his favorite jeans and a starched white shirt and headed out to meet Mary Grace.

He saw her first.

Nervously patting the little bun that grazed the back of her neck with one hand and straightening her dress with the other, Mary Grace walked carefully across the sand in her new white sandals to their arranged destination. Two bright blue umbrellas blew gently in the wind above teak lounge chairs, bookending a small bistro table topped with a chilled bottle of champagne and glasses. The resort's PR magician, Kelli Langford, had set things up exactly as Mary Grace asked, and her potential beau was standing by the table grinning from ear to ear.

As she approached, Mary Grace extended her hand and Vince took it in his, with a small gentle shake. Her hand felt so tiny, almost childlike, and it immediately put him at ease. Mary Grace smiled, and then smiled wider, as she looked into the open face of this Belle Meade billionaire dressed in faded worn-out jeans.

And he looked great.

Popping the cork on the champagne, Vince was impressed that Mary Grace had taken the initiative to try to charm him. It was certainly working. She was prettier than her photo even though it stood out in the Rewind Profile Binder left in his room at check-in. He had pressed a Post-it Note on her page with a triple star on it after reading her profile page. She sounded compassionate, cute, and kind, three things that really appealed to him.

Never a pageant princess or a CEO, Mary Grace only aspired to be a voice for those who had none. She longed to right as many wrongs in our society as possible, be generous and kind to everyone, and help build a system that provides an equal education for everyone. She knew she was lucky to be born into a privileged family, in a free country, and be educated in the best schools.

It just didn't seem fair that it was all by chance. That there was no effort on her part to have such abundance when so many people lived in hopelessness and despair through no fault of their own. It was life's lottery simply based on luck. It needed to change.

Her first reaction to seeing him didn't go unnoticed.

As they watched the waves ripple toward shore, he described his love of building things; of taking an architect's creation and figuring it out mathematically. It was like being a dream-maker, the magic of seeing it all come together from paper to reality. His firm had engineered dozens of skyscrapers all around the world. They had offices in Nashville, Singapore, and Geneva and were known for their innovation and inventiveness.

Vince and Mary Grace were amazed at the things they did have in common. They fell into easy conversation as the sun set over the mountains of ash, as the flames from tonight's limbo party began to light up the sky, and Chubby Checker was piped onto the beach with his oldie hit *Limbo Rock*. The silliness of it all made them laugh, and they gathered their things and headed down the shattered shell path toward the crowd forming on the shoreline.

The resort was providing large, chilled pitchers of Sangria, and shrimp stacked with pineapple skewers to eat. But knowing that a splendid dinner awaited them at 8:00 pm, Mary Grace and Vince declined the many trays of colorful canapes passed under their noses. Instead, they watched with amusement as guests, including Margot and her favorite date Arthur, tried their best not to knock the limbo pole off its stakes, forgetting that at least sixty years had passed since they tried the very same thing on their school playground. But it was all in good fun, and as the crowd grew tired of falling backward into the sand, fire dancers and brightly masked drummers wound their way down the dunes to entertain them.

While milling through the crowd, Mary Grace and Vince bumped into the gang from the pool party the night of their arrival. After polite introductions and a bit of teasing about their efforts to win the limbo contest, Mary Grace asked if anyone had spoken to Arnie. His suitemate mentioned that he had been turned away at the Aloha Medical Center and was told that Arnie was recovering brilliantly, but would require physical therapy to strengthen his legs and perfect his gait, given the change in his lower limbs. This sounded reasonable to the group, so nobody questioned why Arnie was unable to have visitors.

"It was part of the agreement," they were told, "when they filled out all the registration forms upon resort acceptance." Mary Grace felt uneasy about Arnie's situation but directed her energy toward her first and fantastic match date with Vincent Blalock. Curious, Vince asked about the circumstances and was perplexed, as well, that this Arnie could have no visitors. He hoped that it was the Aloha Medical Center's attention to minimizing the possibility of infection. Vince remembered when his late wife came down with a terrible infection and her unit's medical team was garbed in hazmat suits, he wasn't allowed to visit either.

He also hoped that Arnie wasn't any competition.

Vince steered Mary Grace to the reserved golf cart that was ready to drive them up the volcano's side to Ash, the resort's most expensive and exclusive dining establishment.

Watching the fires from the limbo party below, the newly matched couple nestled in to a table on the modern, moon-shaped balcony overlooking the ocean. It was absolutely beautiful. An impeccably spoken waiter, in a crisp black tux, approached them with a warm greeting and the wine list. Vince asked Mary Grace's preference and found a lovely bottle of pinot noir for them to share. She was not a big drinker, and the champagne on the beach had done the trick to calm her nerves. Now she had to be careful and not totally embarrass herself on this monumental and magical first date.

After ordering an appetizer, the two were amused as they both chose a Caesar salad and veal piccata for their meal. It came with a side of fresh spaghetti aglio e olio. It couldn't have been more delightful. Mary Grace hadn't eaten that much food in one sitting in years, she realized, but was so focused on Vince that her plate was totally cleaned before she knew it. The service was attentive without imposition, and the two talked and laughed and learned their separate life stories and what brought them to Rewind Ranch.

Mary Grace explained about her condo tribe and how they met for coffee each morning, lamenting the lack of male companionship in their lives. Vince felt his charitable contributions had made him a sitting duck for the single women attending those events with an eye on his bank account rather than him. He wanted to meet someone that knew only what he was, not what he had, and that money was never part of the picture. His late wife had been his college sweetheart, and they grew financially together.

The fact that she had loved him for him was never a question. But ten years on the Silver Sneakers dating scene had educated him on the new rules. A great many women wanted to see his financial statement before 'wasting their time'. It was only when he had an appointment with a plastic surgeon to schedule surgery on skin cancer that he saw the resort brochure and picked it up. He figured this was his chance to get rid of a few wrinkles, take a much-needed vacation, and perhaps meet someone with whom to share his life.

Vince wasn't desperate; he was determined. He wanted to find someone who appreciated but wanted to share what they had, as well as live the simpler way of life in the country. He wanted someone who loved horses and dogs, walking at sunrise, and savoring the sunset. But his large estate and private plane gave a false impression of Vince, one most women didn't care to understand, much less pursue.

So he tended to spend time with his male friends and neighbors, despite their celebrity. They were nice people, creative and talented, and understood his passions. And they too supported the organizations for the underserved communities in Nashville and made sure they had access to food, shelter, and training for a better way of life.

Mary Grace breathed in deeply, letting the air out in a slowly paced breath. Totally satiated, she drank the last bit of pinot in her glass and gently placed it on the table.

"This has been wonderful," she remarked.

"More than wonderful. I am so blown away that the resort matched us so well. At least, I think so, and hope you do, too, 'cause I would really love to see you again."

"I'd like that."

"I'd like that too," Vince softly stated as he motioned for the driver to bring up the cart. Vince reached for the back of Mary Grace's chair and led her to the driveway, his arm around her smooth shoulders. As she turned to face him, he gently leaned in and kissed her gently on the forehead.

"I'll go inside and settle up. The driver will see you to your door. I'll call you tomorrow."

As the driver turned the trolley to proceed down the hill, Mary Grace turned to watch Vince saunter inside the spectacular building, his hands once again in his pockets. He walked slowly, consumed in thought, but quickly turned and caught Mary Grace's eye. With that, a wide grin covered his face, and she too smiled in response and quickly turned back in her seat, embarrassed that she had been caught watching him.

'Well, well, well, Mr. Vincent Blalock of Belle Meade, Tennessee,' Mary Grace thought, *'you just might be a keeper.'*

Meanwhile, Margot was hurling up watermelon margaritas in the koi pond.

Arthur was doing his best to hold back her hair and not get sick himself. They had downed the drinks nonstop in between turns at the limbo pole, determined to beat the more limber singles basking in the rowdy crowd's applause. Her stomach rebelled as she was squatting under the bamboo pole, and realizing what was about to happen, she sprang quickly up, knocking the pole across the sand and her head as well. A large purple egg was slowly forming as she ran toward her room, with Arthur trailing behind her. When she got to the bridge, hovering above the slowly swimming, shining scaled koi, Margot lost it.

In an instant, she actually felt better until she realized what a horrible scene she had made in front of Arthur, her number one match. Margot started to cry. Arthur pulled a crisp white handkerchief from his pocket and wiped it under her eyes. She looked like a raccoon with black mascara smeared from her cheeks to her chin. Finding a clean corner of cotton, Arthur wiped the sides of her mouth and the bottom of her face. With that, he leaned forward and kissed the top of her messy blonde hair. "You're a real mess, Margot Meadows," he whispered, "but you're my mess, if you'll have me."

Margot swiftly stood up straight in shock and turned her head to look into Arthur's eyes.

"Is that a proposal?" she asked.

"It is," he whispered. "If I can still want to kiss you after watching you throw up in the freaking fish pond, it's either love or I've had too many margaritas. And that's not the case."

Chapter 14
The Harvest Queen

Margot couldn't wait to get back to the bungalow with the news.

She'd done it; found that handsome Prince Charming that would carry her away from the monotony of 777 Wexford, and propel her into a world where she will be pampered and promised that *happily ever after*. Arthur was perfect, something she recognized that very first night. Wildly attractive, accomplished, and articulate, he was also a lot of fun.

The weeks ahead would be so much fun planning their nuptials and deciding where to honeymoon, and later settle down. But Margot had not forgotten her entry into the Harvest Queen contest, something she had her heart set on winning. And if she did, she and Arthur could spend as much time here in paradise as they wished, free of charge.

She had penciled in the first contestants' meeting in her black suede day planner weeks ago, but here it was, set for lunch tomorrow. Margot wanted to make a good impression and had brought her white silk Armani pantsuit for this special occasion. Accessorized with her nude stilettos and Temple St. Clair Byzantine gold earrings, Margot should obviously outshine the other contestants there.

She just wasn't sure what the criteria for judging would be. No talent contest, thank God, and they were a bit over the hill for a bathing suit competition, she hoped. *'Maybe,'* she thought, *'it would all be based on looks and popularity with the other guests, providing that they were actually judging.'* It was all a mystery, but one to be soon solved.

As she entered their mini villa, Margot was met with the news that Lacey Ann was back in the med center for tests. Her back pain was worse, and they wanted to check for a possible infection under the skin. Before Mary Grace had accompanied her there, she made Lacey Ann promise to look for Arnie and see what was going on. She had a bad feeling about his care and hadn't heard a word since she sent the balloon bouquet.

Maybe if Lacey Ann could just talk to him for a few minutes, they would all have a better understanding of what was happening, and why nobody was allowed to see or even phone him in that outer-space-age monument called a hospital.

When Lacey Ann checked in, she was informed that Dr. Lei was no longer working at the resort and the new and stunning physician, Dr. Wu, would be taking over her recovery. This news came with much appreciation since communication with Dr. Lei was so very difficult.

Lacey Ann was escorted to the third floor of the Aloha Medical Center by a stoic blonde dressed in a crisp white tunic. Her room was pristine, with a lovely window view of the harbor, and she enjoyed watching the boats float in and out of the small bay leading out into the Pacific. After changing into the traditional white caftan, Lacey Ann surveyed the dinner offerings and chose to have a large bowl of chicken and wild rice soup and a buttered croissant. Her tests would begin in the morning, they said, and Dr. Wu would be by sometime this evening to explain her plan and Lacey Ann's schedule for tomorrow.

In the meantime, she wandered out to the Client Comfort Center to see the other patients, and perhaps figure out a way to inconspicuously get upstairs to Arnie's room. Mary Grace had remembered his room was number 418, so she presumed it was almost directly above her room, which was 318. Each floor had a comfort center, which consisted of a living area with a giant flat-screen television, a community dining room, and a small office that housed six computer terminals with office supplies, but unfortunately no Internet. Additionally, there was a masseuse, hair stylist, and nail bar, so the guests could look and feel their best. Lacey Ann returned to her room to lie down.

Her back was still hurting. She would be so glad to get this pain taken care of so she could get on with finding her perfect match. Honestly, lying in a hospital, no matter how beautiful, was not Lacey Ann's idea of a vacation. Luckily, Dr. Wu showed up right after Lacey Ann finished her dinner, and sat on the side of her bed to talk.

As earlier suspected, she also thought there was some type of bacteria causing Lacey Ann's pain. She had ordered a blood test, a CAT scan, and a steroid infusion to boost her immune system. When they received the results of the blood tests, she would add the appropriate antibiotic.

With no further surprises, Lacey Ann should be good to go in three to four days max. That gave her some tangible encouragement. For the first time in weeks, Lacey Ann felt that soon this nightmare would pass, and she would be able to join in the fun and put her energy toward being matched and meeting a dashing new suitor who would sweep her off her feet.

After a long day of being poked, prodded, and photographed, Lacey Ann waited for Dr. Wu to explain the results of her tests that evening. She had noticed that the nurses did add another drip to her infusion pole; obviously, it was another antibiotic to cure the bacteria pulsing through her tiny body. When the beautiful physician finally showed up after dinner, she explained to Lacey Ann that the pain was the result of her body healing from the rather extensive liposuction needed to extract enough fat for her now lovely breasts. In essence, only time and painkillers would take care of her problem.

Lacey Ann, somewhat distraught, didn't understand how liposuction could be so painful for her and not her bungalow mates who were now having fun forging new relationships and enjoying the paradise for which she had high, high hopes. She was being watched for another few days, so Lacey Ann decided to put her energy into finding Arnie and trying to ignore the fire coming out of her badly bruised back.

It was almost too good to be true.

As she was doing her daily stroll down the hall with her favorite nurse, a stretcher appeared exiting the elevator, and Arnie did a quick double-take as he passed Lacey Ann. With one hand motion, she knew something was amiss. Arnie's left hand emerged from under the sheet and motioned to Lacey by making a strained claw. His eyes displayed total fear.

It was so disturbing that Lacey Ann knew she would have to find Arnie before something ominous happened to him. He had been in here for over two weeks. And by the look of his pale face, Lacey Ann knew he wasn't doing so well as they had been told by both the chiseled receptionists in the lobby as well as their eternally euphoric PR princess. Kelli Langford.

Lacey Ann returned to her room, ready for her afternoon nap. The walk had really tired her out, and she quickly slid under the soft, white sheets and closed her eyes. Almost fast asleep, she heard giggling going on in the hallway outside her door. It was Dr. Wu and one of the other surgeons she didn't recognize.

And then she heard her beautiful physician softly say as she tried to muffle her high-pitched laughter as she promptly pinned the 'No Visitors Allowed' sign on Lacey Ann's door. They were merrily discussing her progress or lack of it.

"She has absolutely no idea what's happening."

Lacey Ann was in shock. The thought that her physician was laughing at her after a major operation was horrifying. And what was she referring to? All Lacey Ann knew was that her back hurt from the liposuction. Terrified, she knew that somehow she needed to get out of this secluded hospital and tell the girls that something really unusual was happening.

About that time, a cheerful nursing assistant entered her room and handed her a small note.

"It's from that lovely Mr. Katz upstairs," she said, "I think he may be interested in you!"

Trying to keep her composure, Lacey Ann took the folded note sealed safely in an engraved Aloha Medical Center envelope. As the nurse softly closed her door, Lacey Ann opened the envelope and unfolded the first communication that any of the girls had been able to have with Arnie. She thought the whole thing odd, as it was obvious that Arnold Katz was totally besotted with Mary Grace after the evening by the pool.

And Mary Grace seemed to want to meet him as well. None of this made any sense. With trepidation, Lacey Ann unfolded the crisp white paper. It was oddly written and didn't sound quite like the happy-go-lucky New York bachelor she remembered, laughing and teasing the girls unmercifully. Studying the message, Lacey Ann scoured the curious, carefully crafted print before her. It sounded like a different person had written this stilted and friendless, formal message.

Hello, Ms. Peyton,
Even though we have barely met, I would
Love to get to know you better.
Please respond if interested.

– Arnold Katz

Lacey Ann heard the lunch trays rattling in the hallway as she slipped the note behind her bedside table. It was bothering her, and she didn't know why Arnie would address that to her. Maybe after some lunch, she would take another look to decipher what was so disturbing.

A tall, thin male orderly literally pranced into her room, smiling from ear to ear, and holding a shiny, silver tray topped with the most luscious array of fresh fruit and cheeses imaginable.

"Lunch, ladybug," he warbled, "you're gonna' love it."

With the grace of a dancer, the young man placed the bed tray across Lacey Ann's lap and flashed his pearly whites once again. With that, he gracefully bowed to the floor, brushing his right fingertips in a perfectly airless sweep, belying his ballet training.

"You're a dancer," Lacy Ann gasped.

"Used to be, ladybug, before I broke my ankle in a really bad landing five years ago. I thought I was the new Baryshnikov, until I did something really stupid, chasing the spotlight. It was a hard lesson."

"I am so sorry. I was a dancer too in my younger days. I studied and danced at ABT."

"Those were the days, right?" he said, as he grinned and glided out her pristine white door.

Then she heard the sound of the lock snap into place.

With that, Lacey Ann's stomach lurched. Why would a hospital lock the door? What on earth was going on? Lacey Ann picked at her lunch but devoured the warm, freshly baked cookie that accompanied it. It made her tired, and her eyelids began to droop. It was time for another nap.

One where she too would be chasing the spotlight while dancing on stage, not for the appreciative applause, but for the few special moments she was lost in the beauty of it all. It was like flying across the sky, unaware of her meticulous muscle memory and consciousness of the combinations she had practiced for hours on end for these few priceless, precious, and perfect moments in time.

It only took moments for the sedative slowly dripping into Lacey Ann's arm to take effect. She would sleep for hours now, and give the hospital personnel time to decide whether to continue her present treatment of high-dose antibiotics and steroids or let nature take its course. They would need to consider the ROI as well as the fact that she had come to the island with several close friends. Those sugar-soaked, sweet, Southern women weren't referred to as 'steel magnolias' for nothing. They might cause trouble, something the medical center didn't need at any cost.

The Katz client in room 418 wasn't doing any better; another one of the now departed Dr. Lei's patients taken over by the stunning newcomer Dr. Wu. His bone stretching had increased his stature a record 2 1/2" in height, and he now had the nose of an Adonis, but the additional procedure of inserting his faux six-pack was causing him a great deal of pain.

They anticipated a good round of antibiotics would clear things up, but were concerned he had reached the point of sepsis, and a decision needed to be made about the plan of action going forward. The gregarious New York gentleman had come alone and was scheduled for surgery almost immediately upon his arrival, so his time to connect with many other guests was limited. They knew he had no family back home, and had mentioned he may want to move to the Hana property for the rest of his retirement.

There was a lot to consider, and Dr. Wu had summoned accounting to review his case before she proceeded with any more treatments. She would, however, do another full-body MRI on him that evening to be sure of his overall condition. Then she made a note to check the Global Request Board before rendering her decision.

Arnie lay in bed, sedated by the morphine drip; his mind wandering from one fond memory to another. He sometimes was conscious of the here and now and was praying that Lacey Ann understood what that note was trying to tell her. Something was amiss here. The island paradise that seemed too good to be true was indeed not what he, or anyone, had thought.

Meanwhile, Elli was busy working on the Friday obituary column which had a bigger-than-normal number of clients on it this week. Not many, considering the amount of beautiful but advanced-in-age people wandering around the island, but it seemed enough to catch her attention. Scanning the information, most of the deceased had been housed in the Aloha Medical Center since their surgeries and hadn't had a chance to enjoy their newly engineered looks or meet the matches of their dreams. She surmised this as none had any matches or photos from their Reveal.

'*What a shame,*' Ellie thought. She also made a mental note to speak with her wonderful surgeon, Dr. Meredith Morgan, who assisted on a few of them, and see what she could find out about the casualties. It might shed some light on the problem. Perhaps these people are having too many corrections or have unrealistic expectations.

She knew from experience that everyone was instructed on the possible complications, and had to sign a waiver before they would accept them. It just didn't seem to be a big deal when they were swooning over the entire package of absolute hedonistic ecstasy and a Prince Charming to boot.

Elli did notice that the monthly Crystal Ship excursion was scheduled for Saturday night with two of the three deceased. She quickly scribbled the event on her calendar, hoping that her new beau Scott wouldn't mind the change in plans. Maybe she could just say it was a sunset cruise she noticed on the calendar with some excellent sixties music as the entertainment.

But the big story this week was the Harvest Queen Contest. In a stroke of luck, Shawn, the Feature Editor, had asked if she could handle the story in this issue, and Elli was delighted. She could use her creativity and do some human interest reporting. And the icing on the cake was that Margot was included as one of the ten contestants.

It would be so much fun taking the ladies' photographs and crafting articles about each of them in preparation for the actual event. She could also reveal how the ladies had built their support among the guests and communicate the platform they planned to represent. There would be a surprising senior swimsuit contest and evening gown contest, and the all-important, spontaneous question from the resort judges, who would reveal the contest's top three based on guest ballots, and then ultimately the winner based on theirs.

Elli had already begun to brainstorm props and locations for the photos but was stumped as to how to tie in the contest title. There was no sign of growing gourds or plump pumpkins, so she guessed the harvest was the amazing fruit gloriously growing everywhere around the amazing acres as far as her eyes could see.

'And oh, the vineyard! she remembered, that would be perfect'. Satisfied with her idea, Elli returned her attention to the business at hand, describing the lives of the resort guests who met their demise chasing their dreams. As usual, the remains of those not having a family were to be cremated at the Eternity Center and honored on Saturday night as they sailed across the silent, shining sea with Jim Morrison singing a sad and sexy 'sayonara'.

The sound of her cell phone broke her concentration. It was Margot, gushing about the Harvest Queen meeting and the new swimsuit she just purchased on the plaza for the contest. She wanted to meet for a quick lunch.

"She had to work on her tan," she said, "and get some color on the white stripes left from her previous suit's straps." Why she wouldn't just get a spray tan was beyond Elli's imagination, but that was Margot for you. Plus Elli could suggest her idea about shooting at the vineyard and winery at sunset one evening. The light would be so beautiful at that time.

Margot came merrily walking up to the open-air patio where Elli sat sipping her sparkling soda. "Hey Harvest Queen," she chirped. "Oh, don't jinx it," Margot said, "I really want to win. It would just be the most wonderful gift, next to meeting my darling Arthur here too."

Elli mentioned her vineyard idea but Margot wanted the beach. She managed to get in a concern about the weekly obit column she just wrote, in between Margot's constant musings. It was obvious that her euphoric friend was in no mood to talk about darker subjects. And after eating a small Caesar, so as to not gain weight, Margot scurried off leaving Elli to finish her tuna salad sandwich all alone.

As Elli was wiping the final French fry across the last drop of ketchup on her plate, Mary Grace came by unexpectedly. Just wanting some iced tea, Elli sat with her and talked about how lucky they all were to have met these magnificent men on their vacation, not to mention their successful surgeries. This led to a short discussion about Lacey Ann and their concern that she has missed the entire resort program because of her post-op problems.

Elli mentioned contacting her own doctor, who seemed much more approachable than Dr. Wu, and seeing if she would check on Lacey Ann for them. "Probably not," Mary Grace said, "probably against the rules." But they agreed that they needed to do something, and being banned from even seeing her certainly wasn't helping the situation.

And then there was Arnie, Mary Grace mentioned. He seemed to be having a similar problem and has been isolated the whole time he has been here. It was just feeling strange, and the girls decided to put some thought into getting to the bottom of it. They would find a way to get inside that mysterious Aloha Medical Center if it killed them.

Margot was putting a great deal of thought into her Harvest Queen platform. She didn't want something like 'world peace' or the popular 'green' issues. It had to be something that was emotional to this hedonistic crowd. Something they could relate to personally as they went about their privileged lives, being sought after and successful, and now nearly physically perfect. They were all senior citizens, too; proud of their families and grandchildren, pictures of whom were passed around like the hot hors d'oeuvre tray at every gathering and gala. They were their latest creation, their future of sorts; perfect in every way.

'But what if they weren't?' Margot thought. *'How could they not be moved to tears by children less than perfect; children with no funds to finance the extensive plastic surgery they just received?'* It was at that instant that Margot found her platform. It was sure to be a winner.

And she would present it as Elli's portfolio photographs of children who received free medical treatment from US doctors overseas flashed behind her. Margot could see it all now, and she was elated at the prospect of being this year's *It Girl,* the one and only Harvest Queen.

She had ordered her gown from Rent the Runway; no need to spend money on a one-nighter, especially one from her favorite designer Vera Wang. It was simple and sexy. She could envision herself walking the catwalk in that pure white, off-the-shoulder sheath, contrasting with her perfectly toned, tanned skin. She would wear pure white stilettos and her simple but sparkling, three-carat diamond studs.

The white pantsuit she wore to the luncheon had been perfect. It had raised the perfectly arched eyebrows of all the other contestants. And she thought that stark white evening dress would do the same thing. And, Arthur remarked, she would be ravishing.

There was so much to do. She knew Elli could help write her speech, and Mary Grace would help her with her swimsuit. When you wanted an honest opinion, Mary Grace was the one to ask, and she knew she wouldn't steer her wrong. She was leaning toward her newly purchased, bright red tank, cut high on her lean, lengthy legs but wasn't sure if the red was just too loud.

She wished Lacey Ann was available to help her with her walk, and hoped that maybe she would be released from the medical center in time for a little practice. She wanted to make Arthur proud that he had landed such a catch. It would boost his ego, not that it needed it, and boost hers as well. Margot had her sights set on winning, as always.

Her dad constantly quoted football coach Vince Lombardi to her when she was a young girl. "Winning isn't everything; it's the only thing," he would tell her. No matter if it was a spelling bee or a tennis match, Margot was expected to win. "Show me a good loser and I'll show you a loser," he would always quote through his loud, larger-than-life laugh. No, losing was never an option for Margot.

Mary Grace came through with her suggestion of choosing an orange tank for her instead, cut high on the legs, low in the back, and reminiscent of that iconic Farrah Fawcett poster that hung in every college fraternity house back in the day. It was not only sexy, and enhanced Margot's tan, but just might spark a nostalgic nod in the gentlemen voting for their queen. *'It was a brilliant suggestion,'* Margot thought, and supported the new image with plans to wear her hair down and tousled, while sleeking it back in a neat chignon for the evening gown competition.

And the competition was scheduled for next Thursday night.

The weekend was here before anyone knew it. Margot stayed in the suite writing and rewriting her speech with Arthur by her side. He was her thesaurus and room service liaison, as well as her biggest fan. He loved her platform and found numerous nonprofits that supported her cause. And being an engineer, his technological savvy had Margot's slide show put together within an hour on her laptop. It was all falling together, just like the two of them.

Elli and Scott had a romantic, poolside dinner and then wandered down to the dock to board The Crystal Ship. He had been a great sport about it and was somewhat fascinated by the entire process. It was certainly eerie but somehow fit into the fantasy world in which they now existed. The boat was a beauty, made of solid wood and shined to perfection, and Scott made a mental note to check out similar ships up on the Cape.

The sky was a kaleidoscope of colors, pink, purple, and orange, and the silhouette of the sky-scraping sails against it was beyond beautiful. It was so quiet except for the muffled murmurs of the couples on board, and Scott was so glad he had come. After the burial boxes were slipped below the water's surface, the traditional, tearful song began wafting over the water as the ship began circling back to shore. The crew began tossing the ropes as they approached the elegant boat slip built specifically for the ship, and the couple was back on land shortly after an hour's time. They walked along the shore for a while and then decided to return to the bungalow and see how Arthur and Margot were coming on their Harvest Queen project.

Margot was delighted with Arthur's slide show. His choice of photos, cropping, and timing was perfect. But something was missing. "Music!"

Margot quickly shrieked. "We need grab-your-heartstrings music to the visuals!"

"Like what?" Arthur asked. And so they began thinking and tossing our names of songs that might add the missing ingredient.

When Elli and Scott walked in, they had no idea what was going on. It was like a game of Name That Tune without music. After a brief explanation and reviewing the list Arthur had jotted down, Scott sheepishly said, *"I'll Stand by You."*

"That's it," Margot screamed. "Perfect."

And so armed with a killer dress and a slide show fit for the Sundance Film Festival, Margot strutted her stuff as she did years ago. It was like the pageants of long ago. Assured, articulate, and wildly attractive, it was no surprise when her name was called for the top three. Only the spontaneous question to go, and Margot would win the Harvest Queen contest just like all the baby contests, the high school contests, the college contests, and now in her golden years.

She had written and memorized answers for every current issue she and Arthur could think of; war, peace, education, health, race, women's issues, guns, opportunity, you name it. She thought she had a safe, nonpartisan but intelligent answer for anything. She was the last to be called to the podium after the two previous ladies gave serious but very general answers to very pointed questions. Kelli Langford, who was the emcee for this portion of the contest, offered the large glass bowl with the remaining question to Margot, who gracefully reached in and then handed it to Kelli.

She promptly read from the card that 'the question was twofold, and the first part being how do you play a tactile role in creating a more peaceful world?' Margot promptly described her belief in the Golden

Rule and her random acts of kindness. The audience clapped politely as Margot readied herself for the second question. "What would you say," Kelli began, "to the Dalai Lama if you were given a chance to speak to him?" Margot tried not to look stunned while her brain searched for an answer. Then somewhere from deep within her came her quick, candid response preceded by a big, wide, winning smile. "Well, I believe I'd say Hello Dalai!"

The audience roared. The judges laughed and clapped as they checked their ballots. It was a shoo-in, and Margot won the glass slipper.

She and Arthur were both elated. Margot stepped forward and gently dipped as Kelli placed the orchid lei around her neck after giving Margot a big hug. *'It was a moment in time she would never forget,'* Margot thought, as the crowd whooped and hollered at their new queen. She wanted to pinch herself to be sure she wasn't dreaming.

They announced that the new Harvest Queen and her escort would now perform the first dance of the evening; something neither Margot nor Arthur were really prepared for. But as Arthur walked up to the stage steps, Margot floated down and took his hand. Together they walked out to the dance floor center, passing their smiling friends as they went. The lights dimmed and the orchestra took their positions as they began to play her well-chosen theme song, *I'll Stand by You*. It never occurred to Margot that the lyrics applied to her as much as the daunting, disfigured children whose flashing photos sealed the deal for her.

Chapter 15
Suspicious Minds

The girls were so happy about Margot's success.

They surrounded her with hugs of happiness and a chilled champagne toast to the new Harvest Queen. As she raised her glass, Elli caught a glance of her physician, Dr. Meredith Morgan, in the crowd. Trying to inch her way through the throng of people, Elli finally caught up with the friendly doctor as she was leaving the party to return to her rounds.

After a short, "Hello, nice to see you," Dr. Morgan didn't seem to want to engage in conversation. Determined to help Lacey Ann, Elli followed her outside and gently touched her shoulder as she was boarding the Turtle Trolley, and said, "Dr. Morgan, please, I need your help." The urgency in Elli's voice got her attention.

Elli explained the situation with Lacey Ann, the excruciating pain in her back, and their concern for her well-being. "Could you please just check on her for us?" she begged.

Dr. Morgan explained that it wasn't possible to question another physician's treatment plan, that was professional courtesy at the very least, but if she had a valid opportunity to visit her floor she would stop and say hello to Lacey Ann as a friend. Dr. Morgan stressed that Elli was to tell nobody that she agreed to do this, as she would certainly lose her position on the island. Elli thanked her profusely, agreed, and said she would see her at her check-up next week.

Racing back through the crowd, Elli realized her friends had already left for a celebratory dinner at Ash. Knowing she would have to run her photography equipment back to the office, she would meet the group there, and keep it to herself that Dr. Morgan would do her best to check on their sick friend. She hated to lie to them, if asked, but realized that Dr. Morgan was adamant about their deal. Her job was on the line and Elli knew that.

The dinner party at Ash was in full swing when she arrived. Margot was pouring more champagne into the groups' sparking glasses herself, spreading the joy. It was so nice to see Margot so happy, and Elli couldn't wait to take the annual photos of her and write the article on her win.

It wasn't until Mary Grace and Vince arrived that the subject of Arnie and Lacey Ann was brought up. The guys thought that being isolated in that hospital was very strange, but didn't really grasp the seriousness of their situations. They all politely offered to help in any way they could, although they were all at a loss as to what that would be.

Elli woke up early the next day pumped about working on Margot's photo shoot and coming up with an angle for her feature story. She would have to clear it with Shawn but felt he would be more than happy for her to take it on. She was surprised to see Mary Grace making coffee so early but soon learned that she and Vince had decided to ride horses on the beach before it got too hot. Things were going so well for all three of them, and they constantly were amazed that their vacation was the best decision they had ever made.

Margot was a joy to work with, mainly because she trusted Elli to show her in the best light possible both in the photos and in the article she was cleared to write. They checked out locations, went to the plaza to borrow some fabulous outfits, and checked the weather. Rain was the forecast for much of the week, so the ladies decided to schedule the shoot for tomorrow afternoon after Elli finished her work at the newspaper. They would do one shot in casual clothes on the beach, walking at the water's edge with dozens of island children.

Kelli Langford was able to arrange this by giving a donation to one of the cleaning staff's daughter's school. The children would all be given new book bags for their time. The second shot would be in an evening gown, on the romantic deck at Ash with the setting sun in the background. The third would be Margot and Arthur at an indoor table at Ash.

'Easy peasy,' Elli thought, *'what a far cry from the winners of the tennis tournament last week, thank God.'* Seems the wives of the double pairs were all decked out in party curls and jewelry and looked so ridiculous in their tennis skirts that Elli had to talk them both into dumping the jewels and the curly coiffured wigs.

The afternoon at *The Inside Scoop* was lighter than usual, so Elli took the time to do a little research on the Aloha Medical Center. It was financed by the National Bank of China, the country's largest financial institution, and it was built by Manchu Construction Corporation headquartered in Beijing. It made sense now to Elli why so many of the surgeons came from Asia. Some of the surgeons had been schooled at Guangzhou Medical University and their train-abroad program, sending students to Johns Hopkins, Harvard, Duke, and the top hospitals and med schools in the United States.

She then started looking at the medical center administrative staff and their employment histories. Strangely, none of this information was available anywhere, and Elli had to really dig to find any information on most of them. The ranch on Instagram featured the glamour aspect, before and after photos of the transformations, photos of the Reveal fashion event, and a myriad of shots of young-looking old people having the absolute time of their lives. The campus shown was a sprawling arrangement of modern structures set within the pristine white sands and turquoise waters of Hana.

It was spectacular. Elli did notice for the first time that back behind the Aloha Medical Center, where the Eternity House was positioned, was a heliport where in this particular shot, three unmarked helicopters sat waiting for their next journey. *'Interesting,'* Elli thought, *'that they weren't offered rides from the airport in those, rather than the stomach-churning drive on the Hana Road.'* But she had not remembered seeing the helicopters fly since she had been staying in Hana and made a mental note to pay more attention.

As the sun lowered in the sky, Elli began gathering her equipment and readied herself to meet Margot on the predetermined sandy strip of beach they selected for the shoot. She hoped the stylists were on time, and had prepared Margot for her first shot. No need to have her hair styled for that, as her tousled hair would be a plus. She would photograph Margot and Arthur afterward as they were meeting up for Wellfleet oysters and champagne at Ash for dinner. It was amazing that with the choice of daily activities, Elli hadn't gained a pound after eating all this glorious food for weeks on end.

'Now that's paradise,' she thought.

As she left the building loaded down with equipment, her cell phone rang. Unable to answer it, she quickly glanced to see if it was Margot or something else of importance. She would call whoever it was back tomorrow. But the name that flashed at her was Dr. Meredith Morgan. Trying to balance the office Nikon between her chin and chest, Elli did her best to reach for the phone in the back pocket of her jeans but didn't answer on time.

She would check later for a voice mail hoping to hear that Lacey Ann was doing well and would join the group soon. She caught the Turtle Trolley at the flagged corner stop and made it to the beach just in time to see Margot treading down the dunes loaded down with casual clothes for their first shot. She looked beautiful, and soon the sun lowered in the sky and produced a ravishing sunset as the backdrop. Arthur had arrived to watch. They were a dashing couple, and they could have been featured on the cover of *Town and Country*.

Kelli Langford texted that she and the children were on their way down to the beach and were ready to have their photo taken with the queen. Margot jumped into the cabana's colorful restroom and changed clothes quickly. Dressing in white pants, rolled at the hem, with a crisp white shirt, and her hair peeking below a sassy straw bowler, she looked adorable and perfect for the shoot.

Kelli looked a bit overwhelmed for the very first time to Margot and Elli. She was being circled by two dozen children running and hollering. It almost looked like she was being burned at the stake, but Elli, who was used to working with them on shoots, immediately got their attention as she described their important role in the queen's feature story.

As they clustered around Margot's long legs and strolled the beach with her, what was once total chaos became magic. Elli couldn't wait to see the film later that evening and edit the shots. The other shots in the evening gown and with Arthur proved to be just as stylish and stunning. Elli was impressed at the resort's stylists' professionalism and great taste. She wondered if they had been in the magazine publishing world too at some point in their careers.

Work finished, the two, tired 'Wexford run-a-ways' returned to their bungalow, almost too exhausted to dress for the fresh oysters they were invited to partake at Ash. But in true Margot fashion, she quickly reminded Elli, "At our age, you should say 'yes' to everything!"

Approaching the large lemon-colored floral display in Ash's foyer, Margot and Elli joined Arthur, Scott, Mary Grace, and Vince squealing with delight about the photo shoot. Elli had taken a few snaps on her phone and passed it around for everyone to see. When Scott handed it back, she noticed there was another call from Dr. Morgan. Excusing herself from the talkative table, Elli grabbed a lounge chair across the pool deck and dialed Dr. Morgan back, who answered on the first ring.

"Elli, I'm so glad you called," she said. "I can't talk right now, I'm with a patient, but would love to see you later if you're free."

"Of, course!" Elli answered. "Just text me when you're available."

Elli decided not to mention the conversation with anyone until she heard what Dr. Morgan had to say. She surmised it was important and was beyond disturbed, hoping against hope that Lacey Ann was alright. She just couldn't imagine how something sinister was happening under their noses while they were having the time of their lives.

'Too much crime TV,' Elli thought, as she silently scolded herself for overreacting. But she couldn't concentrate on her friends or the fun at

hand, so after devouring a dozen fresh oysters, she excused herself from the table and headed back to the bungalow to wait for Dr. Morgan's text.

It came exactly at 9:00 pm. 'Meet me in the ladies' room at the pickleball courts'.

It couldn't have been a more obscure location. Elli checked her campus map and found it close to the fire pit near the beach. It would take her about fifteen minutes to get there, so she grabbed a sweatshirt, checked that Mary Grace and Margot were still by the pool, and headed out the door.

Dr. Morgan was pacing along the line of gleaming white sinks when Elli entered. She could tell immediately that all was not fine when the good doctor whispered, "Something's wrong."

Chapter 16
Message in a Bottle

Meredith Morgan soon felt as if she had been dropped into a Nancy Drew novel. She was aghast, although had the good sense to maintain her doctor's demeanor when the nurse practitioner on the third floor of the Aloha Medical Center announced that Lacey Ann's door was locked per the hospital's rules for 'Pending Patients'. Dr. Morgan had never heard that term in any of her other hospital positions, even during her residency, but acted like it was business as usual. Requesting a consult with Dr. Wu, the newest physician she had yet to meet, it was curtly communicated that the new doctor would not discuss her Pending Patients with anyone.

Determined for more information, Dr. Morgan returned to her office and tried to access Lacey Ann's records, but the files were marked Confidential: Access Denied. With that, she tried scanning the patient roster to see if any other patients were classified as Pending and found Lacey Ann listed along with Margaret Henson Cantwell, Jonah McKinney, and Arnold Katz. All of the Pending Patients were assigned to the renowned and rude Dr. Wu.

She didn't know what any of this meant but thought she would jot the names down and see what she could find out later about their procedures and conditions. And, she would let Elli know that something was amiss with Lacey Ann's isolation but would be careful not to frighten her any more than she was. The Aloha Medical Center had an exemplary record and was regarded as the best in the country for elective surgeries, so there must be a logical explanation for all this. She had a patient on the same floor, so her plan was to watch the comings and goings of the staff when she could, and possibly slip into Lacey Ann's room behind them.

Elli, who was gasping for air from her run to the pickleball court, could hardly catch her breath when she heard Dr. Morgan's concern. Hearing the whole, suspicious story of her third-floor visit didn't help Elli's sense of panic rising in her throat like a raging river. Dr. Morgan tried to calm her with the same reasoning she used on herself. She promised Elli she would try again soon and report back any news, reminding her that their sleuthing must be kept totally confidential.

Elli returned to the bungalow, slipping in unnoticed. She didn't know if she felt better or worse. She trusted Dr. Morgan and was grateful she was willing to help, but felt unnerved about the staff's reaction to her visit. Quickly undressing, Elli lay in bed trying to figure out what she was going to do.

Meredith Morgan was doing the identical thing in her cloud-soft bed at the physicians' quarters on the other side of the resort campus. Each villa was built in quadrants with four physicians in each of the fifteen bougainvillea-covered buildings. Because of their long hours and need for rest when home, the doctor's private quarters consisted of a bedroom, study, bathroom, and kitchenette. The main kitchen and dining area were in the building's center and staffed with a professional chef that made and stored fresh meals for them daily.

It was a fabulous idea and kept the medical staff well-fed, rested, and healthy. She was so happy to be selected for her position here and didn't want to jeopardize it in any way. But she found the hospital's protocol disturbing and prayed there would be a simple and sensible explanation for the secrecy surrounding the Rewind resort's Pending Patients.

The next morning, both women rose early, showered and dressed, and went to their respective jobs as the sun was rising over the ash-covered mountains. Both had a mission, both were running on adrenaline, and both were determined to get to the bottom of it.

A break came as Dr. Morgan was checking on her third-floor patient, and Dr. Wu happened to be in surgery. A code blue was announced to room 318, Lacey Ann's room, and Dr. Morgan rushed down the hall. Lacey Ann was having respiratory difficulties, so Dr. Morgan instructed the nurses to administer oxygen to ease her breathing.

Once settled, and the nurses left the room, Lacey Ann opened her eyes as Dr. Morgan softly said, "Elli sent me." With that, Lacey Ann slowly reached from under the covers and searched behind the nightstand for the note from Arnie. "Give her this," she whispered, "there is something wrong happening."

Hearing footsteps, and an angry Dr. Wu's pursing lips cursing at the nursing staff, Dr. Morgan quickly slipped the note into the empty water bottle on Lacey's nightstand, picking it up as she did. As Dr. Wu came roaring into the room, Dr. Morgan quickly updated her on Lacey's condition and promptly left before Dr. Wu could grill her as to what on earth she was doing in her Pending Patient's room.

In haste, Dr. Morgan turned down the wrong corridor and happened upon a meeting of sorts where several doctors were discussing the patients listed on a huge whiteboard titled Global Requests. Seeing her in the hallway, they quickly slammed the door.

Rushing back to her office, Dr. Morgan breathlessly plopped into her ergonomic swivel chair. Grabbing her Yeti, she took a serious swig of cold water to calm herself. She wondered why she had even gotten herself into this senseless situation, except that she really liked Elli, and knew from their conversations she was no drama queen.

And the look on Lacey Ann's face haunted her. The girl was obviously not only sick but scared. Something was really wrong and her curiosity and concern had put her in a really tough situation. She didn't want to jeopardize her job but was compelled both personally and professionally to help Lacey Ann and Elli.

As luck would have it, no surgeries were scheduled for this afternoon, so hopefully, after rounds, she would be able to run by *The Inside Scoop* office and give Elli the note. Then they can talk about their carefully concealed next steps. In the meantime, Dr. Morgan would see if there was any way to access Lacey Ann's charts on the computer and try to get some information from the nursing staff on the third floor. She would also look into that rude Dr. Wu's background and see why she seemed to have such power at the medical center.

The staff seemed as frightened of her as Lacey Ann was. Freshening her lipstick, Dr. Morgan grabbed her files for the day and began her rounds. Luckily all her patients were doing very, very well, and she had several almost ready for their big Reveal. This was the fun part of her job; watching her patients respond to their transformations as she removed bandages and braces. It was so very rewarding, and she could not imagine doing anything else.

And, with the state-of-the-art technology here at the Aloha Medical Center, she was able to do things faster, safer, and better than she ever had anywhere else. She was so thrilled with her offer, which allowed her to not only live in a paradise totally rent-free, but she had unrestricted access to dine in four and five-star restaurants, and unlimited classes and concerts during her free time.

It seemed like everyone here at Rewind Ranch was living their dream. But she began to wonder if some unfortunate guests were living their worst nightmares.

Elli tried to concentrate on the business at hand. She had finished researching the conception and development of The Crystal Ship and had begun writing about her experience on the ship's last voyage. It would be three weeks before it would sail again, so she hoped her notes would cover all the questions she had about the monthly journey. She wanted to portray the experience as somewhat mystical rather than sad, so as not to dissuade other guests from participating in the sunset sail.

Her new love interest, Scott, had really enjoyed his time on the ship, finding it relaxing and romantic. Having recently begun to sail himself, the vintage wooden ship was absolutely fascinating. It was a different feel as they glided across the glassy sea; heavier and more stable, although the journey provided the same soothing silence as they headed toward the horizon. He thanked Elli for suggesting the trip and wanted to do it again when it sailed next month.

Elli was polishing her opening paragraph when Dr. Morgan came through the sleek glass door to her office. She looked disturbed, which put Elli immediately on edge.

"Did you see her?" she immediately asked.

"Yes, but just for a minute. She looks scared, Elli, and not well. She said to give you this."

Dr. Morgan handed Elli the crumpled paper note. She quickly opened it, filled with trepidation, and was concurrently confused when she saw it was from Arnie.

"Why would Arnie send Lacey Ann such a weird note? We all talked and laughed with him for hours our first night here, and he definitely had a huge interest in Mary Grace."

"Let me see that," interrupted the curious surgeon. Dr. Morgan read the note aloud trying to decipher why the note was written so peculiarly. She read it a second time, and then a third. She stared at the words, the letters, the phrasing of his message, and his lower-case signature.

Then she saw it.

"Oh my God, look Elli! He wrote the word HELP with his capital letters. He needs help. Oh, Elli, something really strange is going on over there. We need to figure this out before someone gets hurt."

Elli felt nauseous. She was sure Lacey Ann was in trouble, and she had to figure out a way to get her out of that hospital before something really terrible happened to her. She shut down her computer and packed her things while Dr. Morgan looked on helplessly. Without speaking, they both knew that they were companions in this mystery, and they needed to go somewhere and develop a plan to find out what Dr. Wu and that steel monolith on the hill were up to and figure out how to stop it before it was too late for poor Arnie and Lacey Ann.

Before they could get out the door, Shawn strolled in surprised to see Dr. Morgan in Elli's office. "What's up?" he asked. "Just doing an interview for an article you are going to love," Elli said through a

Cheshire cat smile. "I should have it ready to show you next week at the latest."

"Awesome, Miss Alabama," Shawn laughed, "What on earth am I going to do when you leave this place? You have spoiled me rotten. I may have to get approval to add you to the staff for good if you're not careful."

"Well, that's the best offer I've had all day," teased Elli back.

"Just dropping off another listing for your Friday back page obit. No rush. It's a short column this week anyway, which I guess is a good thing, right?"

"Well, not for the people I'm writing about," Elli automatically answered as she waved her file folder marked OBITS. "Specifically, Margaret Henson Cantwell and Jonah McKinney."

"Don't forget this one," Shawn said, sliding the new folder across Elli's desk. "Arnold Katz."

Chapter 17
The Eternity House

Elli felt like someone had just punched her in the stomach.

Dr. Morgan gasped and then tried to cover up her horror in front of Shawn by pretending to suppress a cough and clear her throat. Quickly excusing herself with a fictitious appointment, she briskly walked out of the Media Center and headed for the beach. Her head was pounding, and she had to think. She needed desperately to find out Arnie's cause of death, the real cause of death, without causing any suspicion.

She wondered if he had family or was a permanent resident and if his body was destined to be shipped home or cremated here on the island. She was sure Elli or her friends would know some of that, but a friend in the Eternity House morgue would certainly be helpful. She had met a renowned pathologist at one of the new associate mixers and had talked to him at length. Maybe, just maybe, he could answer some of her questions without raising any eyebrows.

She wasn't naive enough to think that if something sinister was going on that providing there was an autopsy, the pathologist would either be in on the reality or somehow sheltered from actually performing it. And, if the attending physician assigned a legitimate cause of death, there would be no need for an autopsy, which would most likely be the case. But he might have access to files that she didn't have, and access to parts of the Eternity Center. So a conversation certainly wouldn't hurt. She would make the call to Dr. Michael Tenley tonight.

Elli's hands were still shaking as she locked the door to her office. How would she tell the ladies that Arnie had passed away? They all would be devastated and feel like they hadn't done enough to save him. And then, how will they get to Lacey Ann, who was being watched like a prisoner behind locked doors, and the fire-breathing physician Dr. Wu?

Sending a group text, Elli asked that everyone meet at the pier as soon as they could, the men included. She would have to figure out how to protect Dr. Morgan but make them all understand that Lacey Ann's life was on the line, and they needed to get her out of the medical center and off the island. When the group figured out the reality of their fantasy island, they would realize that they all needed to get out of Hana, which had more danger than a tiny twisted road.

Dr. Michael Tenley, the new pathologist, was delighted to hear from Dr. Meredith Morgan. She had impressed him the evening of the new associate mixer with her educational background, her career record, and her sense of compassion for those she treated. Hoping this was a personal invitation, rather than a professional one, he ardently accepted and suggested they have a glass of wine by the pool that next evening.

Plus he was so glad for the break from the boredom he felt at a job where he performed so few autopsies. Having previously been a medical examiner for a large Midwestern city, Dr. Tenley was used to working feverishly every day, trying to understand and solve the question of how his patients met their demise. He loved his job. He loved the process of solving the puzzle that could bring both closure and justice to so many people.

At Rewind Ranch, he had only performed one case so far, while his senior and harried partner, Dr. Raul Garza, had been assigned and performed all the rest. And the heavy-lidded doctor, who was so cheerful and energetic during his interview, avoided conversation with him now and rudely refused any help with his heavy workload.

Dr. Morgan was more interested in access to the Eternity House and what actually happened there. She had noticed the helicopters again taking off on Thursday evenings, one after another. They were always back by Monday morning, obviously traveling at night like three shining rockets on the Fourth of July, that began side by side and then when they hit a certain altitude, would drift in different directions.

One rarely saw them in the air during the day. She also was curious if an autopsy was done on Arnie or any of the patients featured in the next obituary column, and if so, what cause of death was actually recorded. Elli had mentioned that they were continually told how well he was doing every time they inquired.

Meanwhile, she planned to find out what on earth a Global Request Board was, not usual for any medical institution in which she had ever worked. And what in the world was a Pending Patient? She had so many questions she hardly knew where to begin, but Dr. Michael Tenley might help her decide what to look into first, and even might give her a friendly tour of his office and the lab. If she could just get inside that building without causing suspicion, she might be able to learn what was going on in there and also understand its mission.

"You look lovely! It's great to see you again," Dr. Tenley exclaimed as he stood up from his seat at a small table for two located a few yards behind the diving board. It immediately put Meredith on edge, as it wasn't the professional greeting she had hoped for. But Dr. Meredith Morgan wasn't dumb. She knew that a little flirting can go a long way when dealing with the opposite sex.

"Thank you," Dr. Tenley, "it's great to see you, too."

"Oh please call me Michael. It would be nice just to hear my first name again."

Meredith had to laugh. The stiff social protocol on the island called for professional titles at all times. The fact that he actually broke the rules gave her a hint of hope.

The conversation revealed that their experience at the resort so far had been vastly different. Dr. Morgan's schedule was packed, and she was challenged and motivated. Dr. Tenley said he had only performed one autopsy since his arrival, and he was, "No pun intended, bored stiff."

Appreciating his sense of humor and easy manner, she commented that there had probably been almost a dozen deaths since they both arrived two months ago, which seemed unusual. Usually, with multiple surgeries, the cause of death is not immediately known unless sepsis set in. And the Aloha Medical Center had a spectacular score on its infection rate.

"Dr. Garza is slammed, and he refuses to let me help him. I just don't understand why they recruited me to sit around all day and twiddle my thumbs. I'm thinking about calling Human Resources and seeing if they can help. If it doesn't improve, I'll resign. So, let's talk about something other than work. What would you like to drink?"

Meredith leaned forward, rested her chin on her hand, and prepared to ask the big question. "Did you happen to autopsy an Arnold Katz?"

"Well, since I've only done one, it's easy to remember. That would be 'no'. It was a woman who obviously had a massive stroke. Kind of a textbook case, really. I'm honestly not sure why they even asked for one, now that I think of it. She didn't go upstairs to the crematory but was transported home in one of our 'signature' coffins."

Meredith didn't comment on his frustration and sarcasm. He seemed to be as much in the dark as she was. But he had access, and that was what counted.

"Then I'll have a 'signature' Bloody Mary," she said with a grin, "and hold the blood."

After their second drink, Meredith and Michael had relaxed into easy conversation, talking about their childhoods and hilarious 'coming-of-age' stories. Both were studious, socially awkward, and shy, but bloomed in college, and later excelled in med school. Drinks turned into dinner, and then coffee. They agreed to meet again soon.

"Where would you like to go next time?" he asked as they were parting ways.

"The Eternity House," she shouted back, as he shook his head and grinned.

"From here to eternity?" he yelled, waving his arms and loudly laughing as he sprinted up the hill like a ten-year-old schoolboy.

She actually liked him. So much for keeping a professional posture. But she got what she came for, and couldn't wait to see the impenetrable interior of that sphinx-like structure sitting high up on the hill. She just knew in her soul it had something to do with the unusual mysteries she had seen in the Aloha Medical Center: the locked doors, the dour Dr. Wu, the Pending Patient sign dangling on Lacey Ann's door, the fear in her eyes, and that haunting, daunting note written by the now-deceased Arnold Katz.

Dr. Morgan was overwhelmed with what she had seen and dreaded what was to come. Hands shaking, she returned to her suite thinking the whole way that she had made a terrible mistake accepting this position. When something seems too good to be true, you can bet your life that it is.

Elli's feet felt like lead as she walked down to the pier.

Once everyone was gathered out above the ocean, where nobody could overhear their conversation, Elli took the note Arnie had written to Lacey Ann out of her pocket and reluctantly read his cry for help. Softly taking Mary Grace's hand, she told her friends that Arnie had passed away and that both she and Dr. Morgan feared that Lacey Ann was in danger. They didn't understand what was going on, but they had to make a plan to get Lacey Ann out of the medical center and back home. And depending on what Dr. Morgan finds out, they all should ready themselves to quickly leave the resort, too.

Devastated but determined, they divided into two groups; the ladies would develop a plan to get Lacey out of that horrific hospital, and the men would plan to get her home. They would meet the next night at dinner with their ideas and try to develop a plausible escape. As the group departed, their demeanor had totally changed. Without a word being spoken, each knew what the other was thinking. What on earth had they gotten themselves into?

After a restless night, Dr. Meredith Morgan checked her phone before dressing for work.

Zipping up her starched white tunic, she wondered how long it would take Dr. Tenley to extend an invitation to tour the Eternity House.

Standing five stories tall, she wondered what would be housed there in addition to a pathology lab, a crematorium, and a mortuary. By noon, she was a bundle of nerves and considered calling him on her lunch break, but luckily he had the same thought. "Tacos and a tour tonight?" he asked. "Bueno!" she replied.

In order to not arouse suspicion, Meredith made a professional call to his office and made a 5:00 pm appointment to discuss a patient. His sassy secretary scheduled the meeting with an added warning that if she was late, there would be no entering the building. The guards left at that time, and there was no admittance except for Eternity House employees.

Meredith charged her cell right before leaving her office in case she had the opportunity to snap a few photos. She felt like a private investigator sneaking around like this, but there was too much on the line to back out now. Taking a deep breath, she locked up for the night and headed up the hill. As she walked closer, the size of the building seemed much smaller, less imposing. It was tall but narrow, with a false front that made it appear much larger from below, and hid two large porte cocheres, one on each side. She could see the chimneys on the far end of the roof, with the rest of the space, she surmised, used as a heliport.

The guard was peeking at his watch as she approached the entrance but quickly checked the monitor for her name and destination. He asked her to look straight into the screen for a facial recognition check and rang Dr. Tenley's secretary to announce her arrival. Walking past the building directory, she noticed the departments listed, with the crematory on five, an ICU on four, Pathology on three, Global Fulfillment on two, and the vast lobby on the first floor.

World news was being flashed on the disarmingly large flat screens that covered its walls. It reminded her of Wall Street's World Stock Exchange trading floor minus the frenzied, pale-faced brokers screaming into their phones. Oddly, she still felt the same menacing tension.

She entered the sleek, silver elevator and was whooshed to the third floor.

Dr. Michael Tenley stood smiling at her as the doors glided open. She was actually glad to see him again, but couldn't let her emotions sidetrack the business at hand. She already had questions after seeing the building directory, especially the function of the Global Fulfillment department on two. She had seen something similar written on the formidable whiteboard in Dr. Wu's hospital wing.

Dr. Tenley walked her around the offices, but most doors were closed. He said that floor two was not accessible to him, but they could walk through the ICU and his lab as a start. The pathology lab was pretty typical, all shining stainless steel, with a small wall of refrigeration drawers, sinks, and scales. The ICU was composed of a dozen suites, a large nurses' station, and an unusual wall of monitors that resembled an airport flight information screen. Dr. Tenley had no idea what it meant any more than Meredith, so she silently sneaked a snapshot to study later. The walls of the rooms were glass; looking into the nurses' station, Meredith could see that most of the patients were sleeping peacefully.

Michael Tenley suggested they go for a quick peek on five and then they head to Juan in a Million for some tacos and a margarita.

As the doors opened on five, the crematory was to the left behind a sturdy steel door, and an unmarked entrance was to their right. There was a daunting No Admittance sign as well as another facial recognition plate by the door. Somewhat perplexed, they heard a rolling cart roaring their way and jumped aside as a young maintenance man rounded the corner pushing a laundry cart full of soiled scrubs and surgical gowns.

Meredith and Michael looked at the dirty laundry and then each other simultaneously, both wondering what and why surgery was being performed in the Eternity House and not the hallowed Aloha Medical Center. Meredith exited the ominous building with more questions than answers.

Chapter 18
The Man with a Plan

Dr. Michael Tenley's days suddenly became more interesting.

His evening with Dr. Morgan had left him disturbed and distressed, with the exception that she was someone he would like to pursue. She was not only attractive, but smart and caring, and didn't suffer fools, just like him. She was determined to help Elli and her friends despite her high salary and position at the resort, and Dr. Tenley felt the same way. There was something really strange going on, and his pathologist's brain was on it. Another puzzle to be solved instead of actual surgical work in the lab. And Dr. Tenley loved to solve puzzles.

He knew the ladies were working on a plan to get Lacey Ann out of the medical center, and the men were working on a plan to get her off the island unnoticed. He would take on the 'why' of it all. What was going on behind the fashionable facade of fabulous that the resort offered to these senior citizens? He wanted to know who funded this 'pretend paradise' and what they got out of showing a colony of older, wealthy singles the time of their lives. *'Follow the money,'* he thought. *'It is the most direct path to an answer.'*

But before he started snooping into the big picture, Dr. Tenley wanted to check out something he noticed but did not comment on when he and Meredith walked through ICU. It is customary in all hospitals to place the patient's name outside their rooms, not just for protocol purposes but so the staff can call them by name to ease the stress of not being in control. The ICU had something different. It was a series of numbers and letters that identified them, not their names. And, Dr. Michael Tenley wanted desperately to find out why.

While Michael Tenley was seeking out answers to the Eternity Center like a half-starved bloodhound, Mary Grace was searching for Arnie's cause of death. It was just so sudden after being told how well he was doing, and that didn't add up. She decided to make an appointment to speak with Kelli Langford, who insisted all along that Arnie was healing like a well-trained canine. Her demeanor must be one of concern and not suspicion, which would be a challenge, and the thought of putting on her sweet Southern airs brought bile to her newly taut throat.

As Mary Grace began focusing on Arnie's final demise, Elli and Margot were planning on making an appearance at Kelli Langford's office too, something Dr. Morgan suggested, and inquiring as to Lacey Ann's condition while insisting on visitation rights. Margot had read the contracts they had all signed, and there was no mention of their inability to be informed on Lacey Ann's exact medical condition, prognosis, and treatments being performed in the Aloha Medical Center by that viperous, pinched-lipped Dr. Wu. Mary Grace was vehement that doing so was illegal in the United States, and they needed to relay that in no uncertain terms.

Meanwhile, Kelli Langford, perched on the very edge of her ergonomic chair, was concerned that she was perspiring through her sunflower-yellow silk blouse as she nervously typed an email to the home office. Those Birmingham women were starting to upset her gravy train, nosing around the medical center and asking way too many questions. Usually, the pampered pleasure seekers can be subdued with a little face-to-face and a few free margaritas, but not this bunch. They made another appointment today, so playing it safe and sending a heads-up to corporate sounded like a very good idea.

It was unfortunate that Kelli liked the ladies because she might have to present the resort's protocol somewhat sternly and dismiss them like histrionic schoolgirls. They wanted to meet with the Patient Advocacy Center about Lacey Ann, who'd been placed on the Pending Patient list, once her former surgeon, Dr. Lei, was replaced by the newly recruited, resident Ice Queen, Dr. Wendy Wu.

As Elli and Margot marched into Kelli's office like malcontent majorettes, Kelli grabbed a glimpse of a return email thanking her for her expedient communication. She smiled to herself like a satiated Siamese as she motioned for the ladies to have a seat. Offering coffee first, she routinely asked about their comfort before sitting back down, ready for the oncoming confrontation. Margot started in with the restraint of an enraged rattlesnake, demanding to know when they could see Lacey Ann.

Gently patting Margot's arm, Elli appealed to Kelli's sensitivity and concern for her friends. She reminded Kelli that Lacey Ann had been isolated ever since she entered the hospital, just days after her arrival, and a friendly face would do her good. She had no opportunity to enjoy any of the resort's fine dining, events, and accommodations after paying a fortune to do so.

Nor had she met any sophisticated and single suitors, as described in the brochure. They wanted nothing more than for Lacey Ann to have the exquisite experiences they were having here on the island. It was a once-in-a-lifetime opportunity for all of them, and they felt sure there was something Kelli could do. Begrudgingly, Kelli agreed to try. She would email Dr. Wu and ask for some action. As the ladies left, Kelli typed a red-flagged message to Dr. Wu, "EXPEDITE 11407-LK."

Meanwhile, Mary Grace had put her big-girl attorney panties on and began asking questions about the resort operations and owners. Most employees were clueless, but a few long-timers had seen groups of gray-suited gentlemen led around by Kelli Langford, whose cheek-splitting smile looked as if she had a clothes hangar lodged in her mouth. The men were always of foreign descent and mumbled a litany of short-sounding syllables as they pointed and paused by the resort's seemingly unending attractions.

One seasoned sailor took a group on The Crystal Ship excursion early after opening, and it was one of the gentlemen who suggested they add Jim Morrison to the journey. Inevitably they ended up at the Eternity House, where they spent countless hours before boarding one of the three whirlybirds nested on the roof, and flew off into the night sky. One of the fashion stylists, she also learned, was asked to accompany one of the visitors to dinner, and told Mary Grace you'd think she was with the King of England.

The waiters were so nervous, you could almost hear the glassware clinking as they served before-dinner drinks. Hours later, as they strolled the beach and she politely fought off the arms of the aging octopus, he drunkenly murmured to her that he could wow her pants off with insider information about the property. She left him swaying in the shallow surf with her pants intact.

Mary Grace gleaned all she could short of becoming obvious.

She now knew that the resort was owned by a conglomerate hailing from Central America and Shanghai, and financed through the National Bank of China, known to be the most powerful bank in the world. Two of the men had college ties, and the others were somewhat shadier. One was suspected of Cartel ties, and the other was charged but not convicted of human trafficking.

Maybe Arthur could shed some light on any of the owners and how they were turning a profit on such an adventure. Operating costs had to be mammoth, and as a brilliant financier, Arthur would certainly know how to get to the bottom of it. She knew he and the boys were working on an escape plan once the girls figured out how to get ahold of Lacey Ann, but didn't know any details as of yet.

And she was interested in learning from Margot and Elli what Kelli Langford had to say about all this, and if she had put in a requested meeting with the Patient Advocacy Center for them. Glancing at her watch, Mary Grace headed for the Juice Bar to meet up with Dr. Morgan. Hopefully, the good doctor had talked with her new pathologist friend, Dr. Michael Tenley.

Dr. Meredith Morgan appeared nervous as Mary Grace approached the raffia-roofed hut that housed the popular place for healthy juices and ice-cold smoothies. Seated at the end of the bar, Mary Grace slipped silently onto the stool next to her, noticing she had barely touched the glistening green glass in her right hand. She slowly stated the things she had learned from Dr. Tenley and emphasized the three that really concerned her.

First and most important was that additional surgeries were being done in the Eternity House. This was highly unusual. Secondly, most doctors there were forbidden to enter the second floor, nor knew what really happened there. And, lastly, those autopsy assignments were regularly fed to the aging pathologist while the recently recruited and highly paid Dr. Tenley routinely had no work.

There was also the Patient Pending label on Lacey Ann's hospital room door. Nobody yet could identify what that actually meant. But it had become obvious that those patients had been assigned to Dr. Wu when entering the medical center. Dr. Morgan had one of her previous patients labeled Pending when he began running a fever after a simple facelift. Her authority after that was removed, and she was never able to check on him before he left the hospital. Dr. Morgan had hoped to run into him on campus, but that never happened.

Mary Grace took it all in and planned on sharing Dr. Morgan's concerns that night at dinner. Dr. Morgan promised to try again to see Lacey Ann later that evening during the work shift where she would be less noticeable and more likely to gain access. She would text them later.

With a quick and grateful goodbye, Mary Grace headed back to the bungalow to see what Margot had accomplished in her absence.

Upon entering the foyer, Mary Grace thought for just a second she had the wrong cottage. Standing there in front of her was Margot, aka Birmingham-born Nurse Ratched, swathed in a crisply pressed, white tunic and nurse's cap, grinning from ear to ear. In her right hand, Margot clasped two more Aloha Medical Center uniforms and two starched, brilliantly bleached white caps.

"I made friends with the lovely lad in the laundry," she said, "so sometime soon, we're going to pretend it's Halloween in Hana."

Arthur soon rapidly rapped on the tawny teak door moments later. Margot had called him over to show him what she had accomplished that day. He had been busy himself, convinced that the powers that be at Rewind Ranch would somehow need to be distracted on the night they planned to rescue Lacey Ann from her med center prison. The men had thrown around several ideas, but all finally agreed that they would best fall for a plan that involved money.

Arthur had offered to approach the CEO with a donation of a $30 million dollar, state-of-the-art music hall so that they would have a venue for world-class entertainment. The only catch would be that his and Margot's names be on it; a legacy of sorts to the magical place that brought his darling new fiancée to him. He could alter architectural renderings from a past project and prepare a first-class presentation along with Vince, who could present and answer questions regarding construction. They were certain they could grab and maintain their interest for at least an hour. But not much more.

He continued with the men's plan. While he and Vince detained the big-wigs, Scott would wander down to the beach, then to the dock and prepare The Crystal Ship for a special sailing. The girls would have to get Lacey Ann and themselves down to the ship at the appointed time.

But, this Saturday, they all would need to attend the sailing, not just in honor of Arnie, but to intently take in the workings of the ship and how long it would take Scott to sail it to the Hana Airport on the northeast side of the island. There, they would jump into Vince's plane, and he would fly them back to the mainland where they would go straight to the hospital with Lacey Ann, and then to the authorities.

It was a complicated plan, but it utilized everyone's strengths and that was all they really had. They would have to leave everything so as to not cause any raised eyebrows, not that many of the guests could do so. But there was so much to learn, to practice, and to execute without error, and time was not on their side. Before long, Vince and Scott showed up and once Elli was home from work they would start making a task list and timeline.

The telephone broke the strained silence, and Mary Grace, expecting to hear that Elli would be late, was surprised to hear from Meredith Morgan. Breathlessly she said, "I just went to visit Lacey Ann. I couldn't go in. But now there's a number on her door instead of a name. It read 11407-LK. And I got a better glimpse at that gigantic Global Board, whatever that is. And that number is listed on it with a date. It's dated next Tuesday. I'm scared."

Dr. Michael Tenley all of a sudden had plenty to do.

He had accessed some previous patient records of those now deceased and was beginning to chart information about them. He thought he could find a pattern that could lead to what those crazy patient numbers meant. Meredith Morgan had left him an urgent message to call her, and he needed to see what has transpired, hoping she wanted to get together again. But he was well aware that there was Lacey Ann to think of, and getting her some real medical help away from this mysterious island.

He had a lunch meeting with one of the new doctors he meant to cancel once he started his charts, but in his immersion into his findings, he forgot to cancel it. And he ended up really glad he did. The new physician, who hailed from the East Coast, was mystified at his assignments. It seemed that all of his patients were the easy cases, those whose physical exams showed they were well-suited for the surgeries they requested.

Any complicated cases or cases that caused concern, were always assigned to the few foreign surgeons whose workload was extremely excessive. Dr. Tenley hadn't noticed this when casing the hospital files, but it was certainly something to look into more closely. It would also explain the powerful and portentous presence in the medical center of that cold and condescending Dr. Wendy Wu.

After lunch, Dr. Tenley decided to pay another visit to Lacey Ann, or at least her floor, to see if he could learn anything else before returning to the lab and calling Meredith. He wanted to take a look at those numbers again, and possibly peek at the patients in the rooms to see if he could see any correlation. He hoped Dr. Wu, by chance, was away at lunch, thinking it would probably be a plateful of raw meat.

Miraculously he passed the Ice Queen marching out of the building like a determined drill sergeant as he entered. Without even a nod of recognition, she plopped into the Turtle Trolley and demanded that Rubio take off immediately, leaving a few hungry doctors behind. Dr. Tenley figured he would have a safe thirty minutes to snoop around before the beast returned to her lair.

The floor was relatively quiet at noon, probably due to the staff's much-needed lunch breaks. Dr. Tenley sauntered down the hall, not to appear in a hurry, with his phone in hand, to snap as many of the patient numbers as possible. This way he could study them later for a pattern. The patient's gender didn't seem to be indicated in the numbers, but he thought it odd that the first letter of each was either R or L.

As he rounded the corner of Lacey Ann's hallway, he slowed down and buried his head in a chart he brought with him. A passing young nurse he had never seen before nodded in a quick greeting as he stopped at Lacey Ann's door. There he saw her number, 114077-LK taped to the small window. He had a brief and peculiar thought that if someone looked through it from the room's interior, it would look like a mug shot.

Looking up nonchalantly from his chart, the nervous doctor quickly looked down the hall. The coast was clear so he placed his perspiring palm on the slick stainless door panel and pushed. As the door slowly swung open he gasped.

The bed was empty. It had been recently changed and made with crisp cotton sheets and a matching white wool blanket. The edges were perfectly folded like a high-end envelope. As he let the door close, he trembled and turned, as the young nurse was passing by. "Oh, doctor," she said, "114077-LK moved an hour ago to the Eternity Center."

Dr. Tenley called Meredith. Luckily she was with the group, and he headed straight to the bungalow. Elli was on her way home from her office. They all had insidious information to share with each other, and it was obvious that they only had a few days to pull off their enterprising escape. They were all stressed; you could cut the tension with a scalpel.

As Dr. Tenley entered, the room was buzzing with half a dozen conversations all going on at once. It was obvious the girls were on the verge of panic, and the men were trying to calm everyone down. Finally, Arthur took control of the alarmed group, except for Mary Grace who was having a full-blown, Southern 'come apart'. Vince took her in his arms as Arthur began explaining the logistics and learning needed to pull off the plan.

Scott, for one, had to learn to sail The Crystal Ship, while Vince and Arthur had to be adept at being deckhands. The girls had to be believable nurses and pray nobody recognized them. Dr. Tenley offered to get a gurney and Arthur had already had his architectural drawings revised to resemble a style fitting the resort's environment. He would call the CEO tomorrow morning and make an appointment to offer his more-than-generous donation.

Hopefully, the management would be thrilled at his offer and schedule the presentation right away. He would tell them the money needed to be donated before the end of the year for tax purposes, and he wanted to get started as soon as possible. Dr. Morgan would make an appointment with Michael Tenley, and they would locate Lacey Ann's room in the Eternity Center.

They would have to, at some point, figure out a reason for the three faux nurses to see her. And, they all needed to sign up for The Crystal Ship's Saturday sailing this week, and somehow get all the information they needed while paying their respects to poor Arnie Katz.

By the time they were through discussing the preparations, both Drs. Tenley and Morgan had decided to leave Hana with the group. Vince had a ten-passenger plane waiting which allowed room for them. Once the resort discovered the group was gone, they could be in real danger. But Dr. Tenley was getting ahead of himself. He wasn't through figuring out what the hell was going on in his lab.

Chapter 19
The Final Cut

It would be a miracle if they pulled this off.

Michael Tenley returned to the lab to try to decipher the numbers assigned to the Pending Patients. It became obvious that the numbers were sequential, but the letters confused him. He went back to Lacey Ann's chart. Her pain and scar were radiating from her left lower back. She had complained about it ever since her surgery, which was noted as where they liposuctioned fat to construct her new breasts.

Normally, once the bruising disappears, so does any pain, so outside of an infection, the doctor was curious as to why antibiotics were never dispensed. Arnie's chart revealed that his pain was in his chest and his back, but not near his heart. It was on the right side, and the chart reflected that there was a problem with his six-pack implants, which had become inflamed and later infected. But, just like Lacey Ann, his infusions contained absolutely no antibiotics. He decided to take a break and went to the coffee bar down in the lobby where he ran into Dr. Garza on his way out.

"Working late tonight?" the foreign surgeon asked.

"Yeah, just getting organized and learning the lingo around here. Have a good night."

With that Dr. Garza was gone, and Dr. Tenley knew this was his chance to poke around the pathology lab. He had watched the elder physician place his keys in a ceramic dish on his messy desk. Not only were his file keys there, but also the door key to the refrigeration compartments that held the cold corpses waiting for carving. If he could find the patient number and see their actual anatomy, maybe he could unlock what Garza was up to with his constant autopsies.

Micheal Tenley took a deep breath and grabbed the refrigerator key. He studied the assignment board and thought he would first try to examine one body prior to Garza working on it and one after if it was still being held in the lab. And, of course, study the numbers.

The lower left drawer contained patient number 11481-LL. The deceased gentleman had only arrived yesterday and had complications resulting from frontal lipo and chest implants. The scar was fresh, and Dr. Tenley knew he could open it and restitch it without anyone suspecting a thing. Scalpel in hand, he said a quick prayer and an apology to 11481-LL and made the cut.

Spreading the skin, he quickly noticed that some of the ribs had been broken and repaired, which was unusual since the implants usually were placed under the muscle right above them. Using his pin light, he examined the chest cavity inch by inch, moving from one side of the cold stainless table to the other.

With that, he made a startling discovery. Leaning in closer, Dr. Tenley gazed intently and with horror at the large gaping gap where patient 11481-LL's chest had previously housed a left lung. It was gone, freshly removed.

'Of course, he silently chastised himself, the next-to-last letter indicated right or left, and the last letter must represent an organ'. Quickly stitching up the cadaver, Dr. Tenley returned the corpse to its proper place and looked at the list again.

He found patient 114799-H. Quickly repeating his rapid removal of stitches, he was not surprised to see that this lovely woman, who chose to vacation on this beautiful island and elected to undergo surgery for larger breasts, was void of her heart. But she would be rapidly returned to her family, if not become fish food in the swirling Hawaiian sea, with a recorded cause of death as sepsis. His discovery was horrifying, to say the least.

But then something much more horrifying happened. Dr. Garza walked into the lab.

Tenley had finished repairing the incision and was simply closing the door to where the refrigerated compartments lined the far wall. His hand still rested on the door handle although the keys were clutched in his other hand. Garza's head tilted like a curious canine before he spoke in his thick Spanish accent. "That door remains locked when I am not here," he growled. "You hiding a dead body or something?" Dr. Tenley joked, and slowly walked across the room to his desk, slowly slipping the keys into the right pocket of his starched white physician's coat.

Garza headed to the wall of file cabinets and pulled out a thick manila folder. "Good night, Tenley," he muttered as his dark eyes narrowed in studious suspicion, and he walked quickly out the door.

Dr. Tenley wiped his wet brow with the corner of his cotton coat before sprinting across the room like an Olympian track star. Placing the keys in the ceramic dish, he returned to his computer to double-check his theory that those letters represented organs removed from the poor patients who were somehow selected and identified as Pending. Sure enough, the more he studied the charts, there was no doubt that Garza wasn't performing autopsies; he was covering up previous unauthorized procedures with false death certificates.

Tenley dialed Meredith.

He now knew that Lacey Ann was fighting a botched kidney removal and was receiving no antibiotics to fight it. It was as if Dr. Wu was purposely allowing her to get worse, even though the procedure had already been done. Grabbing his laptop, Dr. Tenley raced out the door to warn the others of his frightening findings.

"Not so fast, Dr. Tenley."

He froze as if his world was suddenly put on pause. Two gigantic guards were waiting for him in the hallway, where they slammed him against the slick tile wall and tied his hands behind his back, pushing him into the stairwell. He felt a sharp, searing stab in his neck. For a moment, he felt as if he was underwater; sounds became echoes in his ears.

The guards were talking, but he couldn't process the conversation as his sight began to fade into a tunnel, falling farther and farther away. They were taping his mouth and tying his feet, as they dragged him down the cold, concrete stairs. And then suddenly his world went totally black.

By now, all three couples were squeezed into the lanai reporting any new information they had gleaned that day. Paramount was Dr. Morgan's morbid discovery that Lacey Ann was no longer in the Aloha Medical Center but had been moved to the Eternity House, where by all accounts is the last stop prior to being loaded on the nearest sailing. She had managed to get a closer look at that giant Global Request Board and saw that Lacey's patient number had been moved from Pending to Scheduled. And the scheduled date was Tuesday.

The group was eagerly awaiting Dr. Tenley, who had planned to snoop around the Eternity Center lab and try to glean any information he could about the Global Replenishment Offices on two. Obviously, there was a connection to the big board but it wasn't clear what was actually going on. Arthur had whetted the ravenous financial appetite of the resort's CEO and had garnered an evening appointment Monday to present the plans for the new building.

Vince would be with him to answer construction questions but excuse himself when the financial discussions began. Then he would head to the bungalow to change clothes, and wait for Rubio to take him and Michael Tenley to the ship, later grabbing Arthur, who would wait by the pool after his presentation ended. The girls now had to research the layout of the Eternity Center and locate Lacey Ann. But they needed Dr. Tenley to provide the gurney and help get her out of the building and down to the dock unnoticed.

Meredith dialed him again. It was still on voice mail. The hair stood up on her arms. Looking wide-eyed at her new tribe, she whispered, "Something's wrong. I've been trying all day. We have to go find him."

While Margot, Mary Grace, and Elli stayed to study the elusive Eternity Center floor plans that Vince had bartered from a European engineering company owned by an old fraternity brother, Meredith, Arthur, and Scott headed for the pathology lab to find Michael Tenley. It was getting late, and they all were stressing over how they would get into the building, as they knew the night guard would be on duty out front.

Walking at a fast pace, panic began to set in, and Meredith started to cry. Her tears were interrupted by the sound of the Turtle Trolley zipping up the pebbled path. It was Rubio on his last run of the day. "Get in, amigos," he shouted. "You look like you need a lift." And noticing Meredith's teary eyes, Rubio added, "You also look like you need a friend, senora. Tell Rubio what he can do to help."

With that, Meredith lost it. Rubio's response was so childlike and sincere, so innocent of the terrible things she now suspected were going on in this retched resort. She gathered herself together and asked, "Have you seen Dr. Tenley today?"

Rubio paled whiter than the sand that dusted the floorboards of the Turtle Trolley. He did not speak but was trying to process the proper response. Before he could answer, Meredith also asked, "Do you know if Dr. Garza is still at the Eternity Center?"

Dr. Garza was always the first one out on Fridays, and routinely flagged Rubio down to take him to his sleeping quarters, where he would quickly shower and dress for an evening at Ash, chasing all the small-waist waitresses that served him way too many margaritas. Always overserved, the larger-than-life lech would appear outside at closing with some new server destined to discover she had made a very big mistake.

Garza was a notorious womanizer, and known for his boasting and booze-swilling stories about his family connections to one of the most powerful cartels in Mexico; something one would think he'd keep to himself. Rubio always shuddered when picking him up, and had to bite his lip when Garza ordered him about like a trained monkey, to keep the bile from escaping his throat.

And yes, he had seen Dr. Garza only hours before picking up his unsuspecting guests. He was shouted at by the security guards to take a bound and beaten Dr. Tenley to the cliffs overlooking the north-end beach. There the land rose hundreds of feet above the sand and provided a proper place for the thrill-seeking hang gliders to practice their stomach-churning craft.

Tenley was conscious, but barely, and Rubio knew any word about this from him would result in the same terrifying end. They had left the poor pathologist properly hidden behind a dune, as the hang gliders were out, and they couldn't take a chance on being seen. Their plan was to venture back at night and toss him into the sea.

They had done this before—several times, in fact—as their staff members had either become greedy or suddenly grown a conscience. It's exactly what happened to poor Dr. Lei. Rubio had watched him cry and beg for his life to no avail. He had seen it all and was told he was now an accessory, something he didn't understand. He hadn't slept well since and was determined to get off the island alive.

Sitting up front with Rubio, head in her hands, Meredith, almost whispering to herself, said, "I've been calling all day. Where can he be? Please God, let him be alright." As the trolley entered the pretentious portal of the Eternity House, and crunched its way up the gray gravel path, the friendly driver brought the trolley to a sudden stop.

"He's not here."

All three heads instantly swiveled to face him, mouths agape. Then Rubio told his story.

Before he could actually finish, Rubio threw the cart in reverse and headed for the beach. The sun was setting, and they had to beat the two burly security beasts from finding Tenley before they did. Meredith called Elli and filled her in, trying to keep the panic from rising in her voice. She told her to get everyone organized for the ship sailing tomorrow, and the presentation and escape on Monday.

That was all the time they had left, and they had to make it work. If they could find Dr. Tenley alive, they would have to hide him over the weekend and somehow get him on the ship Monday. It was another complication, but at this point, they had no choice. *'If they pulled this off,'* she thought, *'she would indeed believe in miracles.'*

Of course, Dr. Tenley was not where he was left hours before; that would be too good to be true. However, the sand provided an obvious path to the small ditch where he had crawled. He was half-conscious and severely dehydrated. But the task at hand was to prop him up in the trolley and disguise him as much as possible.

Now shirtless, with Meredith's large Hermes sunglasses and Arthur's Seattle Seahawks baseball cap, Michael somewhat resembled one of the guests that had been in the sun way too long and drank way too much beer. Scott had used one of the ropes to put around his chest and was keeping him upright as the trolley sped along the rough terrain, heading for their bungalow. It was during the ride that Dr. Tenley told them what he had discovered in the lab. Rubio listened intently and then shrieked, "I knew it. Those disgusting bastards!"

Seeing his anguish, Meredith disclosed their plan to Rubio, who had already put his life on the line by helping them. He knew the seriousness of the scenario. As they climbed down the trolley steps, carrying Dr. Tenley under each arm, Rubio turned the sand-crusted key and said, "Do not worry amigos, I will get you to the dock."

The girls had made headway. With a little help from Margot's contact in the laundry, they located Lacey Ann's room on the floor plan.

They were lucky that it was across from the stairwell, but unlucky that they learned another 'surgery' was scheduled for first thing Tuesday morning. It was unclear what the surgery was about, but it was being performed by Dr. Wu and would take all morning, according to the Global Fulfillment Schedule they had uncovered from hanging around the med center and chatting up the nurses.

It was enlightening to them that the Global Request Board covered a wall in the med center and the Global Fulfillment Board and offices were in the Eternity House. Arthur had proven himself to have a somewhat sinister sense of humor, cracking the code of the resort's real agenda. While all the beautiful people were applauding the Harvest Queen and scouring *The Inside Scoop* for their party photos as they laughed in gaiety and drank the Kool-Aid, the joke was actually on them.

The owners and management were making millions by harvesting their organs.

They didn't know how the guests were actually chosen, but more times than not, risky elective surgeries were accompanied by an 'additional service'. An organ was removed if requested by medical teams across the globe. They knew now that Lacey Ann had lost a kidney, a botched job as it was, so she possibly was scheduled to be sacrificed, under the guise of implant removal, for other organ removals to fulfill more global orders coming off the Dark Web. The surgery would, unfortunately, be unsuccessful, and concern over her thin frame, noted on her admission physical, would be blamed.

Of course, the potential guest signed away any liability the resort might have in order to be accepted to this life-changing experience and exclusive opportunity. And they would have access to the best doctors alive. Dr. Garza would then step in to 'autopsy' and record the cause of death and there would be no need for her body to be examined again.

Obviously, Dr. Wu was deeply involved, and Lord knows who else. The group would have to be careful and suspicious of everyone. It was a brilliant idea, kept under wraps, with cosmetic surgeons all over the world handing out their brochures and unknowingly marketing their scheme for a tiny commission. The owners and others involved potentially could make billions if they didn't mind leaving their moral compass at the door.

If they'd ever had one.

When Arthur explained their findings, Mary Grace literally got sick with a wave of nausea, unlike anything she had ever experienced. Margot went white, and Elli sank to the floor. As the seriousness of the situation settled in, Scott grabbed Elli's hand and squeezed it hard, pulling her to her feet.

"I didn't come all this way to lose you," he said, staring into her eyes.

Arthur looked at Margot and said the same. Vince soon followed suit. Then a soft voice came from the couch where Dr. Tenley, wrapped in a monogrammed mohair blanket, had been listening to the horror of this heinous hide-a-way unfold. He gently gazed at Meredith and said, "Me either."

The plan was set. Vince's plane had ten seats including the cockpit. He had to trust that it was checked and refueled as he asked upon arrival. There was no way to get to the Hana airport to check that his instructions were followed. The resort had thought of everything; they were totally isolated from the outside world and were distracted by their egos' insatiable hunger. He was ashamed of himself but couldn't dwell on it now. There was too much to do.

After hours of poking holes in their scheme, the group settled down and had a nightcap. Tomorrow was Saturday, and they had to ensure Lacey Ann was okay before they boarded The Crystal Ship that evening. Margot and Dr. Morgan would somehow check on Lacey Ann, while Dr. Tenley stayed hidden from Garza and his goons.

At 5:00 pm, the three couples would board the ship to learn everything they could, as they said farewell to Arnold J. Katz, the kind and friendly man who had found a fierce fan club among the guests, but had lost his life in the process. Dr. Morgan would stay with Dr. Tenley in the bungalow, developing a plan to get the girls into the Eternity Center on Monday night to rescue Lacey. They had an idea but would need a little help from Margo's newest BFF in the laundry.

As Jim Morrison warbled into the waves, Scott, Arthur, and Vince scanned the inner workings of the ship. Scott had made an effort to talk shop with the captain and effectively became savvy on its operation. He felt capable of carrying out his job with Arthur and Vince as deckhands. As for poor Arnie, the boys felt bad about using his last journey as an eccentric, educational experience, but knew he would understand and also be thankful that they got Mary Grace and the rest off the island. And bring these monsters to justice.

The cheerful captain was more than forthcoming in imparting important information about the prized wooden ship. It was rare that anyone was even interested in it, much less ask questions about its idiosyncrasies and features. He even let Scott steer for a bit, teaching him how to adjust and change course with ease. And the other gentlemen seemed to get a real kick out of learning the ropes, literally, and did a splendid job tying her to the dock at the journey's end.

The captain wished all of his sailings would be so much fun as they grew tiresome and tedious with the half-lit guests routinely requesting the rousing *Light My Fire* after the scheduled somber song. He chuckled to himself and wished poor Jim Morrison could see the lamentable legacy he unknowingly left behind.

The escape plan finally came together. Rubio was scheduled to be waiting for the girls and Lacey Ann at the Eternity Center. He would then swing by the med center for Dr. Morgan, and then to the bungalow where Dr. Tenley and Vince would be waiting to journey to the ship. Then he would head back to get Arthur, before high-tailing it down to the dock. The schedule was tight but actionable, and Rubio was determined to do something good after calmly chauffeuring all these tireless outdoor trips while seething deep inside.

When he delivered the run-a-ways to the dock, Scott would have the ship ready to sail as soon as they jumped on board. Rubio would then drive madly up the mountain as a request for a pickup certainly would now have come from that smug, swarthy sloth Dr. Garza. The perilous plan was on, and now they had to find the courage to pull it off.

Chapter 20
The Body Snatchers

As Arthur finished tightening the double Windsor knot on his pure silk Prada tie, he caught a glimpse of Margot gazing at him in the mirror. He looked so elegant like he just stepped out of the pages of *GQ*, and so at ease with himself. *'Pure confidence,'* she thought. It was part of his attraction, as Margot usually rated her men on the 'three Es': elegance, eloquence, and easy on the eyes.

She'd hit the jackpot on this one and was amazed at his calm demeanor before presenting a truly fictitious donation that would build a world-class performance hall for these soulless scumbags that ran the resort. It was fitting that it was a performance hall, as Arthur was about to perform the role of his life.

"What is it, sweetheart?" he asked.

"You are just so handsome. Sometimes, you just take my breath away."

"Don't say things like that, especially now. You know the risk we're taking."

"I can't think about that now," she said, shaking her head as she pulled the crisp white nurse's tunic over her head. "I am just trying to stay calm and look like a nurse. What do you think?"

"I think you'd look gorgeous in a gorilla suit."

And, with that, Arthur walked out the door.

He wanted to kiss her, hug her, and tell her everything would be fine; that he'd join her on The Crystal Ship before long, and they would sail away to a new and beautiful life together.

But it was too risky; he might get emotional. And Arthur knew he didn't have the luxury of not being totally together, totally confident, totally successful. He envisioned success as he was taught years before. Always predetermining a positive outcome had served him well.

'If you think you're going to lose, you're a loser. Only winners win'. He could hear his father's emphatic voice inside his head to this day, provoking and pushing him to take risks, try harder, and make a difference. *This is by far the most unusual and ultimate risk of my lifetime,'* he thought. Tonight's performance would determine the difference between life and death.

While doctors Tenley and Morgan watched, Margot, Elli, and Mary Grace were pinning their white nurses' caps to their wig-covered heads and making sure their shorts and tanks didn't show through their snow-white tunics. They would have to dump the uniforms and wigs right after they rescued Lacey Ann, and not be recognized. They looked like totally different people, which helped them prepare for the roles they were about to play. Nervous as cats, they left the bungalow one by one so as not to cause any attention.

Rubio was waiting outside to deposit each of them at various walking distances from the impenetrable building. Luckily he had volunteered to cause a ruckus outside with a deafening and stalling engine to divert the guards' attention as the three silently slipped inside the side stairwell door. Because Dr. Tenley was still in hiding, they were unsuccessful in obtaining a gurney, but Margot's laundry contact readily rose to the occasion.

The girls would get Lacey Ann out of the bed, and place her in the rolling laundry hamper positioned outside of Lacey Ann's #11477-LK door. The laundry hamper would instantly be wheeled to the elevator and then out the side entrance, where Rubio would be waiting in the trolley. It sounded so simple, but they knew better.

And they all said silent prayers that they wouldn't run into Dr. Wu. Not only would she question why three strange nurses were headed into Lacey Ann's room, but she was so dangerous, and evidently left her moral compass somewhere else in the world.

The bewitching hour came, and the girls headed out, while Scott tied his deck shoes and stuffed his gloves into his jean pockets. Speechlessly, he left for the dock and the awaiting Crystal Ship. It was dark, and the out-of-the-way paths were treacherous. Slowly, carefully, as he could hear the gales of laughter coming from the Monday night limbo party and bonfire, he crept through the thickets and onto the worn, wooden dock.

Climbing on and taking his station, he began to untie the ropes holding back the ship from the waters waiting for their escape. Scott easily found the keys where they had been stashed after last Saturday's sailing and Arnie's final farewell. Placing them in the ignition, he glanced at the resort with determination and resolve and waited for the others. His breathing was shallow, while his thoughts ran off the deep end. *'What if,'* he thought. He had to stay strong and keep it together.

Arthur was concluding his presentation, artfully aware the bigwigs were trying not to show their greedy grins at his proposal. The architect's rendering was all that was left to show, and the stipulation that he and Margot would be publicly recognized and their names engraved over the pale marble entrance. He had to stretch his comments out a bit, as in his nervousness he rushed his speech, and the girls would need more time.

He had to keep the goons at bay for a solid hour, and then walk nonchalantly to his hiding place by the pool where Rubio would pick him up after getting the others. He was so glad he had on a suit. Sweat was pouring down his back from the tension but wasn't noticeable. It was so unlike him, and somewhat alarming, although he never had so much at stake. It was rare.

As the now-nurses headed up Lacey Ann's hallway, another worker approached them from a small hallway on their left. Open-faced and outgoing, she asked them how they were doing and where they were going. As Margot answered with Lacey Ann's name, she threw her head back and said, "Oh, you're taking her up to surgery, right? They had a last-minute request in the Global Fulfillment Center for a liver just now, and I heard Dr. Wu saying she was going to fill it with this one before they take her heart out. May as well. She's a goner anyway."

"Yeah, she's a goner, alright," said Margot, locking eyes with this cold, callous caregiver.

"They're making billions off these idiots," the friendly nurse retorted as she sauntered off.

Mary Grace and Elli were frozen on the tile floor, each trying to look nonchalant as panic pulsated through their bodies. They continued down the hall but slowed as a nurse's assistant was writing something on

Lacey Ann's identification sign. As they got closer, and the assistant had returned to chowing down on her takeout dinner at the nurses' station, they realized her patient number had changed to #11477-LK/L/H. *'Of course,'* Mary Grace thought, *'first it was her left kidney, and then her liver, and now her heart was to be harvested. How could one place have so many soulless monsters?'*

When Margot and Elli noticed it and realized the sick and sordid significance of the letters and later the Harvest Queen contest, they both wanted to puke. That is when the real fear set in. Not only were these parasites feeding on the final dreams and desires of the older generation, but also they were making billions of dollars and killing people doing so. Mary Grace vowed to take them down the minute she set foot on the mainland. Elli vowed to go national, calling all her media contacts and exposing them to the murderers and maniacs that they really were. No more writing for *The Inside Scoop*.

'Oh my God,' she thought, *'not that too!'*

Lacey Ann thought she was dreaming.

Hearing some scuffling around her bed, she cracked open her heavy-lidded eyes, weighed down by the dangerous dose of Valium they had just given her in preparation for her next surgery. Dr. Wu had promised her this morning that this would definitely end her pain. But there before her dilated, doubting eyes were her three best friends, dressed in some ridiculous white tunic uniforms and a variety of colored wigs. They wore little makeup and no jewelry, and almost all looked like caricatures of their mothers. But Lacey Ann knew those eyes; those clear, caring, compassionate eyes and the sweet smiles beneath them.

"What's happening?" she whispered so softly they almost didn't hear her.

"We have to get you out of here," Margot snapped.

With that, Elli and Mary Grace unhooked all the infusion tubes and grabbed Lacey under each arm while Margot wheeled the hamper into position. They lifted Lacey Ann in and covered her with her three-hundred-thread-count, crumpled-up cotton sheets. Frette, of course.

"Not one word," Margot warned her as she opened the door and headed for the elevator.

Mary Grace and Ellie waited a few minutes longer and then slipped out heading for the stairwell. So far, so good.

Taking the steps as fast as they could, they reached the first-floor exit door just in time to hear Dr. Garza ask Margot what on earth she was doing pushing a laundry hamper outside the building. They froze and held their breath. "Please God, no," whispered Mary Grace. Elli grabbed her hand. But, in typical Margot fashion, she was one step ahead of the white-coated monster.

"Why Dr. Garza, of all people you should know. We have had such an influx of surgeries; we can all hardly keep up. And the laundry staff certainly cannot possibly find out what's really going on here. We all have to pitch in and help each other out, right?" Dr. Garza stared into her baby blue eyes, and then brushed her arm seductively as he continued on his way. "You're a lovely woman, senora," he said.

Lacey Ann allowed herself to breathe. It wasn't easy in the hot hamper covered with crumpled cotton sheets. The 'toot, toot, toot' of the Turtle Trolley broke the silence as Rubio swung into the alley for his first pick-up. Turning the hamper on its side, Lacey Ann cautiously crawled out, and the girls rushed to help her into the colorful cart. Rubio threw it in gear and headed toward the med center where Dr. Morgan was casually waiting at the designated trolley stop.

Her face frozen in fear, she jumped on with the other four ladies and closed her eyes. Down the trail they went, holding on for dear life. The next stop was their white-washed, Bougainvillea-covered bungalow nestled among the lush island landscape. It was such a facade for the reality of the place, all cozy and colorful while those sleeping within had no idea when their number was up, and they'd be down for the count.

And it gave new meaning to the adage they all were told as children, "Beauty is only skin deep. It's what's inside that counts." It was like playing musical chairs to the Death March.

As they pulled up to their front door, Vince and Michael Tenley ran out. Michael clutched a prescription bottle of antibiotics for Lacey Ann to get a jump start on fighting her infection. The kind doctor had also thought to bring Dramamine in case the seas were rough once they passed the buoys marking waters the boat always avoided. Crushed together in the trolley, the terrified group urged Rubio to hurry and get Arthur, and then head for the dock.

Putting his 'pedal to the metal', the trolley lurched downhill, swerving around corners and uneven paths in the darkness. Rubio saw Dr. Garza was texting him, wanting a quick trip home to don his Savile Row suit and grab his favorite bar stool at Ash. There was a smorgasbord of seductresses trying to catch his eye once they discovered he was the chief pathologist and educated at the London College of Medicine.

Though void of any cosmetic surgery, his tawny skin and dark, seductive eyes were a pleasing contrast to his splendidly starched white shirt and perfectly tailored dark suit. He looked delightfully dangerous but definitely doughy. They were absolutely clueless that this provocative pathologist made his living by literally stealing hearts.

Now Dr. Garza was calling Rubio. His phone was lighting up like a Christmas tree and Garza's face was flashing on the screen. It unnerved him. Garza's anger was apparent, and Rubio knew if he didn't answer his phone soon, he would end up in Human Resources being reprimanded like an abused animal. Garza was like that; entitled and arrogant.

The more he thought about it, his distaste and disgust for the man, and this place, grew even stronger. It made him happy to help these people. They were good people, nice people, and it felt so satisfying to finally help someone after realizing the resort's actual agenda.

It was his worst nightmare come true, a Stephen King novel in the making. It was time to circle back and get Arthur. He was hiding at the pool behind the diving board. Arthur jumped aboard.

They were now crossing the sand dunes, edging toward the dock. Everyone was silent, lost in their thoughts or prayers. The sea sparkled like diamonds, stretching ahead like shiny satin as far as the eye could see. The moon was full, hanging above like a red carpet spotlight, and would hopefully light the way to the other side of the island and Hana's tiny airport.

Elli spotted Scott's silhouette first, standing on the dock with the last rope in his hand waiting for them to arrive, and quickly handing it off to Vince as he took his place behind the wheel. The only sound was the water lapping against the wooden ship in the cadence of a ticking clock. They were now nervously listening to the seconds slip away, all hoping to sail to freedom from a vain vacation of enlarged egos and self-love, purchased for an enormous price.

Rubio positioned the trolley as close to the dock as possible. He and Arthur carried Lacey Ann on board first, laying her down gently on a makeshift bed of canvas tarps. She started to cry, overwhelmed by her journey and the return of hope that she just might pull through all this. Rubio tried to calm her, reassuring her that she would be alright, and covering her with his waterproof windbreaker he kept in the trolley in case of rain. The girls helped Dr. Tenley down beside her.

Elli ran to Scott, waiting to finally turn the key and head for the airport. Mary Grace watched Vince untie the rope and jump onto the deck. But there on the beach stood Rubio, the person who actually saved them all selflessly, wanting to do the right thing.

It would be a miracle if he survived, once they were discovered gone, and the powers that be began to piece together how they managed to escape. Rubio wouldn't live to see the place taken down once the authorities were notified and raided Rewind Ranch. They'd never even find his body.

"Farewell, amigos. May God bless you all," he waved from the shore.

The group quickly looked at each other, heads swiveling faster than Linda Blair in William Peter Blatty's *The Exorcist*. They all knew they couldn't leave their newest friend behind. He was one of them now. They all began wildly waving at him to jump on board and join them.

"Farewell nothing, Rubio," yelled Arthur. "Margot and I are looking for an experienced driver. Do you know anybody that might be interested?"

"There's one empty seat on the plane if you want it," yelled Vince. "Hell, I need a co-pilot."

"I have no money, nowhere to go," Rubio responded. "I have nothing."

It was then that Margot saw the flashlights coming over the dunes.

Chapter 21
Aloha Air

With Lacey Ann already lying down on the ship's deck, Arthur told Dr. Tenley to stay put and keep Lacey Ann quiet. He wasn't about to get this far and have it ruined by some suspicious goons trying to strong-arm them into staying in this living Hell. Everyone was to pretend to be partying, acting altered by alcohol, and not panic.

There were three of the intruders and nine of them. Elli began to laugh loudly and was joined by the others. Margot started waving wildly at the oncoming lights. "Come join us!" she screamed. "Party on the dock. Enter at your own risk, Dr. Garza, darling!"

As the lights grew closer, it was obvious that the unexpected guests were Dr. Garza and his two security guards. He began yelling at Rubio. "I've been trying to get ahold of you for thirty minutes, you stupid ass. What the hell are you doing down here partying with the guests?"

"It's my fault, sweetie," cooed Margot. "I invited him to stay, and we just lost track of the time. But now that you're here, why don't you join us? I have been dying to get to know you better and hear about your exciting life in Columbia. You are a fascinating man, Dr. Garza."

"Just call me Raul, please senora," he half-sang in his deep baritone voice; his ego getting the best of him. Their eyes locked and everyone breathed a small sigh of temporary relief.

"You can go now," Garza ordered the guards, now feeling all puffed up. "Rubio, you take them back and never, I mean never, do you not answer my calls. You understand that, dumb ass? I can arrange for that little trolley of yours to run off a cliff. You comprende, senor?"

The fear in Rubio's eyes was only trumped by the hatred he felt for this maniacal monster. He turned and took his driver's seat in the trolley, throwing it in reverse, and almost giving the grinning goons whiplash in the process.

Vince popped the cork on the chilled champagne he brought for the occasion, not realizing that partying with the diabolic Dr. Garza would be part of the plan, but knew the more Garza drank, the easier it would be to overpower him at some point. Arthur and Scott seemed to telepathically know what he was doing and only took tiny sips when necessary to keep up appearances. Margot was in rare form, rubbing the doctor's doughy arms as she softly spoke to him and filled his plastic picnic glass to the brim.

An hour into the worst party in the world, Margot was now sitting in Garza's lap, and Arthur was watching him like a hawk. The guys decided they had to improvise and make a plan to dump him somewhere so they could get on their way. Scott suggested they all board The Crystal Ship and dance to The Doors album on hand for the somber monthly sailings.

Margot screeched in joy, clapping her hands and pointing at the chubby Colombian pathologist. Garza sprang to his tiny overloaded feet and began a stiff and spastic dance. Margot threw her head back in laughter as she remembered *Saturday Night Live* and its 'wild and crazy guys'. It was all anyone could do to keep from bursting into hysteria.

They all carefully climbed aboard, while Scott found the dilapidated tape deck and began to play music loudly on the deck speaker system. Margot began to shake and shimmy, smiling ear to ear. The other girls joined her as they broke into a sexy line dance as Dr. Garza salivated on the sidelines.

The men gathered in the wheelhouse perfecting their new plan as Scott uncorked a fourth bottle of bubbly, handed it to Arthur, and turned the key. The motor sputtered, and then they were on their way; onboard were nine faithful friends and Dr. Garza.

"Plan B, Bro," Scott announced to Vince and Arthur.

The ship roared and began moving toward the horizon. The girls glanced at each other sideways and then immediately focused their attention on the sloshed Dr. Garza trying to keep from sliding out of his deck chair. Arthur brought out the new bottle and poured their special guest another glass as the girls madly clapped and chanted, 'Chug it, Chug it. Chug it'. Garza did just that, then stood to grab Margot by the hips. He faltered and fell.

"Baby doll," cooed Margot, "are you alright?" The ship picked up speed, making it difficult for Garza to gain his balance. "Let's just lie here on the deck and gaze at the beautiful stars," she suggested. With that, she grabbed a couple of throw pillows for their heads and strategically grabbed the fresh bottle of champagne, whispering, "We'll drink to that, won't we darling?"

Garza belched like a wild boar, almost causing Margot to gag. She composed herself and lay down next to him. He put his hand on her bare leg. Trying not to recoil, Margot tipped the bottle to his lips and said,

"Open up, sweetheart," as she poured streams of the smooth, sparkling liquid down his canyon-like throat.

The ship was rounding the corner to the northeast. The lights from the airport control tower were barely visible through the dense fog that had built up since their departure. Arthur and Vince watched the upcoming seas with eagle eyes, aiding Scott in his steering. There were rocks and sandbars to be avoided and compasses to read.

They had to sail as far away from the shoreline as possible, afraid they would be seen by someone on the island. At some point, the ship would be missed, and ranch security would come looking for them.

They talked about Rubio and their concern for his safety. They all hated leaving him but saw no alternative at the time. The goons were armed, and there was no way they could risk it. And they had to get Lacey Ann to a hospital before sepsis took over her entire body and her organs, once destined for removal, would all shut down anyway. The clock was ticking.

Hana Airport was within sight, so Scott steered the boat closer to land. Arthur went to check on the girls and the state Dr. Garza was presently in. Finding him snoring loudly like a black bear, he looked like a beached whale lying on the deck.

Calling for Vince, they carefully lifted him into the dinghy and slowly lowered him into the sea. The tide would take him to land by sun up. Margot ran to the ship's side to take a last look at her stewed suitor and hastily dropped a bottle of aspirin into the rubber boat. "Take that, fat boy," she cooed.

In the distance, sirens blared. Lights all along the shoreline lit up behind them, outlining the resort's manicured lawns and routinely raked beaches. They were almost parallel to the airstrip so Scott accelerated the engine and headed for shore. They had to get to the plane right away. There was a huge jolt as the ship hit the ocean floor, bringing everyone to their senses and Arthur went to grab Michael and Lacey Ann below.

One by one, they jumped ship, waded through the thigh-deep surf to the sand, and began the hike to the airfield. Vince carried Lacey Ann in a makeshift backpack he tied around his shoulders and waist. The trail was thick and wet and filled with insects, but that was the least of their concern.

They finally hit the asphalt, and Vince directed them to his ten-seat PC-24 jet parked in the large metal hangar closest to the tower. He climbed up and lowered the stairs while checking his fuel level and controls. They did their job. The plane was ready for a fast flight across the Pacific, to freedom, once he was cleared for take-off.

Putting Lacey back in the last row, everyone rapidly ran for their seats and strapped themselves in. Vince radioed the tower and was put on standby as they were not expected. In what seemed like hours, the tower radioed that as soon as they cleared the runway, Vince and his clan could be on their way. He taxied out to the tiny airstrip.

There was a rogue luggage cart driving on the runway heading for his position, so security was on its way to clear it and remove the wayward driver. As Vince waited, he thought he saw the luggage cart heading straight for them, the driver waving madly for his attention. Scott, sitting in the copilot's seat, looked closer. Vince eased off the throttle and squinted at the commotion on the runway right below him.

"That's freaking Rubio," he yelled.

Vince ran to open the door and lower the steps for Rubio, scaring the other weary passengers strapped to their seats ready for take-off. Covered in sweat and a little banged up, Rubio sprinted up the steps two at a time. Everyone cheered as Rubio stumbled into the plane and buckled himself into the last seat, next to Lacey Ann, trying to catch his breath.

"I caught a ride on one of the helicopters," he panted. "I told the driver my father was dying, and he hid me in the back with an ice chest full of, well, you know what. The ranch is onto you guys. Garza was spotted by some local fishermen and brought to the beach, and after a pot of coffee, spilled the beans so to speak."

Vince turned around and answered him. "We heard the sirens and guessed the hunt had begun. We've been cleared for take-off so let's get the hell out of here."

About that time the tower radioed them and put a hold on take-off, just as Vince saw six security vans racing up the runway with red lights flashing.

"Hold on, folks," he yelled. "This is gonna be one steep take-off." Vince put the plane on full power, heading straight for the charging cars. As he neared the first in line, he pulled the full throttle and up they went into the night sky, somehow evading the shower of bullets raining vertically toward them from the vans.

Most of the petrified passengers had their eyes closed and grabbed the armrests with white-knuckled grips. As the measured sounds of the gunfire subsided, eyes slowly opened, and they looked around at each other in awe. They had pulled it off. As the plane leveled off and began an easy and effortless ascent above the clouds, the group relaxed into their seats.

Lacey Ann was sound asleep with her head on Rubio's shoulder. Michael's antibiotics were beginning to take effect. Scott had radioed ahead and secured an ambulance for her at LAX. He had also contacted his college roommate who was an informant for the FBI.

They would be sending a SWAT team and several Med Flight planes to Hana that next day. The entire place would be shut down by the end of the week. Then the Feds would two-step in to file charges.

Chapter 22
Aftershock

When they reached safety, there were decisions to be made.

Meredith Morgan and Michael Tenley both decided to move to San Francisco and apply for medical positions there. He was almost immediately offered the position of head pathologist for the city. He purchased a beautiful violet, Victorian flat in Pacific Heights, one of the city's famous Painted Ladies, and began renovating the kitchen and baths. Meredith hoped to help the huge homeless population, and until she found just that, Michael offered her his sun-filled second bedroom. It wasn't long before she moved into the master bedroom with him.

Margot, Mary Grace, and Elli were hell-bent on accompanying Lacey Ann to Cedars Sinai Hospital in West Hollywood. Arthur, being so generous and infatuated with Margot, had reserved a suite for the girls at the Beverly Wilshire Hotel, and also contracted a driver for them. He would return to Seattle to catch up on business and then eventually head to Birmingham to join Margot to help plan their upcoming wedding.

They had decided on moving to Napa and living in the rolling green countryside but close enough to San Francisco where they could enjoy the divine dining scene and evenings at the symphony and ballet. It would be no problem commuting back and forth with Rubio behind the wheel.

Vince would fly home to Belle Meade and wait for Mary Grace to have her things packed and shipped to Tennessee. She planned to keep her condo at The Wexford since Vince could fly her down to see family and friends when she wanted. She had overcome her fear of meeting his famous neighbors, realizing that if they were friends of his, they had to be good people. She actually looked forward to meeting them all.

Elli was happy to become an instant Okie and would call a Realtor to sell her place in the near future. She would trade her Jimmy Choo's for a great pair of cowboy boots and learn to relax and enjoy her life, free of the nine-to-five stress. She spent some of her time writing her first novel, a fictional account of four friends who went on an unbelievable vacation. She eventually would learn to ride and love horses just like Scott and would spend lazy summer afternoons trotting through their acreage in awe of the scenery and the life she now lived.

Lacey Ann Peyton was released from Cedars Sinai a month later. Her infection cleared and her single kidney had responded well to treatment and was operating with the help of dialysis. The persistent pain in her back was gone. All she wanted was to go home. She longed to take her morning walks down Highgrove Park Avenue and grab a cinnamon coffee at O'Malley's.

She missed her Southern mac and cheese and craved grits, fried okra, and Alabama barbecue. She wanted to cheer on the Crimson Tide in the fall and spend long, lazy summers on Rosemary Beach, compliments of her huge trust fund. However, lately, she had been heading west to Napa to visit Margot, Arthur, and her current secret crush, Rubio. Margot watched them with an eagle's eye and could see that they were falling in love. Both had never seemed happier.

It was when landing at LAX that they vowed to reunite one year later to celebrate their new lives and success at pulling off their great escape. They learned through Scott that the owners and management had been charged with illegal harvesting, money laundering, and multiple homicides. They had so many indictments; it was hard to count. It was something to celebrate.

Almost a year later, the formerly tormented tourists booked a block of sumptuous suites at New York's Plaza Hotel. Although they talked several times a month, they were all anxious to see what had transpired over the past year after the elegantly executed nuptials of Margot and Arthur. The intimate wedding was held at the French Laundry in Yountville, just outside of San Francisco in Napa.

Guests were housed at the amazing Auberge nearby, an exclusive end-destination resort. It was all exquisitely done, with Margot's three besties as Maids of Honor and Arthur's pampered pet Pippa as the flower girl. Rubio proudly served as Arthur's best man and checked his pocket every few minutes to be sure the gigantic gem he was to hand over to Arthur was still there.

And now the group was in New York, drawing on the energy in the streets, the melting pot of fine restaurants, the earth-shattering entertainment on Broadway, and the opulent offerings of the ritzy retail stores along Fifth Avenue. The girls were in heaven with the shopping, and the men were fascinated with the diverse but divine neighborhood diners and restaurants.

They consumed the world's best-fried chicken at Red Rooster in Harlem, the biggest Reuben sandwiches they had ever seen at Carnegie

Deli, and the best curry they had ever eaten at Junoon, located close to Madison Square Park. They were eating their way across town and enjoying every second of it.

Of course, the ladies lingered at the designer boutiques, buying up handbags and heels at every stop. They toured Tiffany's and tried on diamonds and rubies, and gushed over the brilliant engagement rings they insisted Lacey Ann try on her delicate fingers. They strolled through Bryant Park, the original home of the splendid Fashion Week shows, and rode the French carousel for a giggle and a glimpse of their carefree childhoods. The couples joined forces at the Metropolitan Museum and had drinks on the Stanhope Hotel's front patio.

They rode a hansom cab across Central Park and took photos by the bridges and fountains, and of all of them singing '*All You Need Is Love*' at Strawberry Fields. Their days were full of love and laughter and wonderment at all the world had to offer.

Tonight, the group decided to go casual and explore the exotic streets of Chinatown. It reminded the girls of last year's trip when they toured San Francisco. They were amazed at the size of New York's colorful community. They were mesmerized by the tiny shops and shopping stalls where Asian men would try to entice them inside.

'Louis and Chanel', they would whisper, 'very cheap'. They wandered through the lantern-laced streets taking in the sights and smells of incense and teas, kimonos and coolie hats, wooden crates of vegetables and fruits, and plucked ducks hanging by their webbed feet ready for roasting. It was a world unto its own, mysterious and mystical.

They had made dinner reservations at Xian, on Mott Street, after Arthur had read a raving review of the establishment's steaming meat dumplings in *The New York Times*. Loaded down with baubles and bags, they walked from Canal Street to the restaurant just in time to make their reservations. A line had already formed outside, and they felt very lucky to get in.

Xian had opened to much fanfare six months prior, praised for its ambiance as well as its food. The interior was splendidly decorated by New York's finest design group, and a world-famous master chef was recently imported from an exquisite establishment in Shanghai. People lined the streets for their delicate, different, and delicious dishes.

The group waited a few minutes by the empty hostess stand when a handsome and charming waiter approached and said, "So sorry for your wait. Our owner serves as the hostess so she can personally greet our guests. She has been detained in midtown traffic. I will show you to your lovely table."

Following the beautifully dressed waiter, they were seated at a large lacquered table with red Scalamandré dragon-print-covered armchairs. It faced a covered courtyard with a luxurious lotus-filled fountain. Replicas of the famously excavated, terracotta Xian soldiers lined the walls as if at attention, and the dishes were sculpted rust-colored terracotta in keeping with the theme. The group was captivated by the detail of the decor and the warmth and sociability of the staff.

After a celebratory umbrella drink, it was time to order dinner. Of course, everyone was dying for the revered and highly regarded House Dumplings. They couldn't imagine coming here and not having a taste. The waiter smiled at the more than obvious order and responded as Arthur requested them for the entire table.

"You will not be disappointed. A most excellent choice, sir."

The happy group had a wonderful time. Conversation flowed like a flower-filled fountain as they reminisced on their previous adventures and looked toward the future. They knew their friendship would last a lifetime. Elli posted a large photo of the meal on Instagram and Facebook before they ravaged the piled-high platters of fabulous food. They savored their supper and declared it the best they'd ever eaten.

Vince immediately texted his neighbors to add Xian to their dining list the next time they were in Manhattan. Scott updated everyone on the FBI findings, their indictments, and search for any of the resort's missing management. They concluded their meal with a large pot of steaming Jasmine tea and laughed as each guest read aloud their fortunes from the exquisitely wrapped, paper-thin, fortune cookies.

Getting up to leave, they elected Elli and Scott to plan next year's reunion, hopefully in the wild plains of Oklahoma where they could rest, ride horses, and roast marshmallows by an open fire, plus dine on Scott's almost-famous barbecue. They talked of hayrides and picnics and fishing in the creek. And sitting out on the porch watching the shooting stars brilliantly blaze across the big, open Oklahoma night sky.

It would be a divinely different week from the fun and fast pace of New York. At that moment, Lacey Ann grabbed her stomach and said, "Oh my God, I feel so sick." She then doubled over in pain.

The group immediately jumped up from the table. As they quickly approached the front of the restaurant, Rubio sprang outside to tell the driver they needed to get to the closest emergency room as soon as possible. At the same time, Meredith rushed to inquire what exactly were the ingredients of the meat dumplings they had all consumed, knowing that would be the emergency room doctor's very first question.

The slim-hipped, Hermes-clad hostess had her back to them as the men helped Lacey Ann out the front door and into the waiting car. Meredith and Margot gently tapped the hostess on her fashionably padded shoulder to ask their crucial question. As the shiny-haired Asian beauty turned to answer, Meredith and Margot gasped in horror. There, as she tilted her pretty head, with her menacing smirk and haunting, heavily lined black eyes, stood the insidious island's gruesome and ghoulish Ice Queen, Dr. Wendy Wu.

"I am so sorry, ladies," she purred. "The meat dumpling is an old family secret and the heart of our success. But I can assure you, it is very, very fresh."